Space Platform

Murray Leinster

Space Platform

ISBN: 978-1-63637-808-4

CONTENTS

CHAPTER 1 1
CHAPTER 2 14
CHAPTER 3 25
CHAPTER 4 38
CHAPTER 5 46
CHAPTER 6 59
CHAPTER 7 72
CHAPTER 8 85
CHAPTER 9 97
CHAPTER 10 112
CHAPTER 11 125
CHAPTER 12 138
CHAPTER 13 148

SPACE PLATFORM

CHAPTER 1

There wasn't anything underneath but clouds, and there wasn't anything overhead but sky. Joe Kenmore looked out the plane window past the co-pilot's shoulder. He stared ahead to where the sky and cloud bank joined—it was many miles away— and tried to picture the job before him. Back in the cargo space of the plane there were four big crates. They contained the pilot gyros for the most important object then being built on Earth, and it wouldn't work properly without them. It was Joe's job to take that highly specialized, magnificently precise machinery to its destination, help to install it, and see to its checking after it was installed.

He felt uneasy. Of course the pilot and co-pilot—the only two other people on the transport plane—knew their stuff. Every imaginable precaution would be taken to make sure that a critically essential device like the pilot gyro assembly would get safely where it belonged. It would be—it was being—treated as if it were a crate of eggs instead of massive metal, smoothed and polished and lapped to a precision practically unheard of. But just the same Joe was worried. He'd seen the pilot gyro assembly made. He'd helped on it. He knew how many times a thousandth of an inch had been split in machining its bearings, and the breath-weight balance of its moving parts. He'd have liked to be back in the cargo compartment with it, but only the pilot's cabin was pressurized, and the ship was at eighteen thousand feet, flying west by south.

He tried to get his mind off that impulse by remembering that at eighteen thousand feet a good half of the air on Earth was underneath him, and by hoping that the other half would be as easy to rise above when the gyros were finally in place and starting out for space. The gyros, of course, were now on their way to be installed in the artificial satellite to be blasted up and set in an orbit

1

around the Earth as the initial stage of that figurative stepladder by which men would make their first attempt to reach the stars. Until that Space Platform left the ground, the gyros were Joe's responsibility.

The plane's co-pilot leaned back in his chair and stretched luxuriously. He loosened his safety belt and got up. He stepped carefully past the column between the right- and left-hand pilot seats. That column contained a fraction of the innumerable dials and controls the pilots of a modern multi-engine plane have to watch and handle. The co-pilot went to the coffeepot and flipped a switch. Joe fidgeted again on his improvised seat. Again he wished that he could be riding in back with the crates. But it would be silly to insist on perching somewhere in the freight compartment.

There was a steady roaring in the cabin—the motors. One's ears got accustomed to it, and by now the noise sounded as if it were heard through cushions. Presently the coffeepot bubbled, unheard. The co-pilot lighted a cigarette. Then he drew a paper cup of coffee and handed it to the pilot. The pilot seemed negligently to contemplate some dozens of dials, all of which were duly duplicated on the right-hand, co-pilot's side. The co-pilot glanced at Joe.

"Coffee?"

"Thanks," said Joe. He took the paper cup.

The co-pilot said: "Everything okay with you?"

"I'm all right," said Joe. He realized that the co-pilot felt talkative. He explained: "Those crates I'm traveling with——. The family firm's been working on that machinery for months. It was finished with the final grinding done practically with feather dusters. I can't help worrying about it. There was four months' work in just lapping the shafts and balancing rotors. We made a telescope mounting once, for an observatory in South Africa, but compared to this gadget we worked on that one blindfolded!"

"Pilot gyros, eh?" said the co-pilot. "That's what the waybill said. But if they were all right when they left the plant, they'll be all right when they are delivered."

Joe said ruefully: "Still I'd feel better riding back there with them."

2

"Sabotage bad at the plant?" asked the co-pilot. "Tough!"

"Sabotage? No. Why should there be sabotage?" demanded Joe.

The co-pilot said mildly: "Not quite everybody is anxious to see the Space Platform take off. Not everybody! What on earth do you think is the biggest problem out where they're building it?"

"I wouldn't know," admitted Joe. "Keeping the weight down? But there is a new rocket fuel that's supposed to be all right for sending the Platform up. Wasn't that the worst problem? Getting a rocket fuel with enough power per pound?"

The co-pilot sipped his coffee and made a face. It was too hot.

"Fella," he said drily, "that stuff was easy! The slide-rule boys did that. The big job in making a new moon for the Earth is keeping it from being blown up before it can get out to space! There are a few gentlemen who thrive on power politics. They know that once the Platform's floating serenely around the Earth, with a nice stock of atom-headed guided missiles on board, power politics is finished. So they're doing what they can to keep the world as it's always been—equipped with just one moon and many armies. And they're doing plenty, if you ask me!"

"I've heard— —" began Joe.

"You haven't heard the half of it," said the co-pilot. "The Air Transport has lost nearly as many planes and more men on this particular airlift than it did in Korea while that was the big job. I don't know how many other men have been killed. But there's a strictly local hot war going on out where we're headed. No holds barred! Hadn't you heard?"

It sounded exaggerated. Joe said politely: "I heard there was cloak-and-dagger stuff going on."

The pilot drained his cup and handed it to the co-pilot. He said: "He thinks you're kidding him." He turned back to the contemplation of the instruments before him and the view out the transparent plastic of the cabin windows.

"He does?" The co-pilot said to Joe, "You've got security checks around your plant. They weren't put there for fun. It's a hundred times worse where the whole Platform's being built."

"Security?" said Joe. He shrugged. "We know everybody who

3

works at the plant. We've known them all their lives. They'd get mad if we started to get stuffy. We don't bother."

"That I'd like to see," said the co-pilot skeptically. "No barbed wire around the plant? No identity badges you wear when you go in? No security officer screaming blue murder every five minutes? What do you think all that's for? You built these pilot gyros! You had to have that security stuff!"

"But we didn't," insisted Joe. "Not any of it. The plant's been in the same village for eighty years. It started building wagons and plows, and now it turns out machine tools and precision machinery. It's the only factory around, and everybody who works there went to school with everybody else, and so did our fathers, and we know one another!"

The co-pilot was unconvinced. "No kidding?"

"No kidding," Joe assured him. "In World War Two the only spy scare in the village was an FBI man who came around looking for spies. The village cop locked him up and wouldn't believe in his credentials. They had to send somebody from Washington to get him out of jail."

The co-pilot grinned reluctantly. "I guess there are such places," he said enviously. "You should've built the Platform! It's plenty different on this job! We can't even talk to a girl without security clearance for an interview beforehand, and we can't speak to strange men or go out alone after dark—."

The pilot grunted. The co-pilot's tone changed. "Not quite that bad," he admitted, "but it's bad! It's really bad! We lost three planes last week. I guess you'd call it in action against saboteurs. One flew to pieces in mid-air. Sabotage. Carrying critical stuff. One crashed on take-off, carrying irreplaceable instruments. Somebody'd put a detonator in a servo-motor. And one froze in its landing glide and flew smack-dab into its landing field. They had to scrape it up. When this ship got a major overhaul two weeks ago, we flew it with our fingers crossed for four trips running. Seems to be all right, though. We gave it the works. But I won't look forward to a serene old age until the Platform's out of atmosphere! Not me!"

He went to put the pilot's empty cup in the disposal slot.

The plane went on. There wasn't anything underneath but

clouds, and there wasn't anything overhead but sky. The clouds were a long way down, and the sky was simply up. Joe looked down and saw a faint spot of racing brightness with a hint of colors around it. It was the sort of nimbus that substitutes for a shadow when a plane is high enough above the clouds. It raced madly over the irregular upper surface of the cloud layer. The plane flew and flew. Nothing happened at all. This was two hours from the field from which it had taken off with the pilot gyro cases as its last item of collected cargo. Joe remembered how grimly the two crew members had prevented anybody from even approaching it on the ground, except those who actually loaded the cases, and how one of the two had watched them every second.

Joe fidgeted. He didn't quite know how to take the co-pilot's talk. The Kenmore Precision Tool plant was owned by his family, but it wasn't so much a family as a civic enterprise. The young men of the village grew up to regard fanatically fine workmanship with the casual matter-of-factness elsewhere reserved for plowing or deep-sea fishing. Joe's father owned it, and some day Joe might head it, but he couldn't hope to keep the respect of the men in the plant unless he could handle every tool on the place and split a thousandth at least five ways. Ten would be better! But as long as the feeling at the plant stayed as it was now, there'd never be a security problem there.

If the co-pilot was telling the truth, though—.

Joe found a slow burn beginning inside him. He had a picture in his mind that was practically a dream. It was of something big and bright and ungainly swimming silently in emptiness with a field of stars behind it. The stars were tiny pin points of light. They were unwinking and distinct because there was no air where this thing floated. The blackness between them was absolute because this was space itself. The thing that floated was a moon. A man-made moon. It was an artificial satellite of Earth. Men were now building it. Presently it would float as Joe dreamed of it, and where the sun struck it, it would be unbearably bright, and where there were shadows, they would be abysmally black—except, perhaps, when earthshine from the planet below would outline it in a ghostly fashion.

5

There would be men in the thing that floated in space. It swam in a splendid orbit about the world that had built it. Sometimes there were small ships that—so Joe imagined—would fight their way up to it, panting great plumes of rocket smoke, and bringing food and fuel to its crew. And presently one of those panting small ships would refill its fuel tanks to the bursting point from the fuel other ships had brought—and yet the ship would have no weight. So it would drift away from the greater floating thing in space, and suddenly its rockets would spout flame and fumes, and it would head triumphantly out and away from Earth. And it would be the first vessel ever to strike out for the stars!

That was the picture Joe had of the Space Platform and its meaning. Maybe it was romantic, but men were working right now to make that romance come true. This transport plane was flying to a small town improbably called Bootstrap, carrying one of the most essential devices for the Platform's equipment. In the desert near Bootstrap there was a gigantic construction shed. Inside that shed men were building exactly the monstrous object that Joe pictured to himself. They were trying to realize a dream men have dreamed for decades—the necessary space platform that would be the dock, the wharf, the starting point from which the first of human space explorers could start for infinity. The idea that anybody could want to halt such an undertaking made Joe Kenmore burn.

The co-pilot painstakingly crushed out his cigarette. The ship flew with more steadiness than a railroad car rolls on rails. There was the oddly cushioned sound of the motors. It was all very matter-of-fact.

But Joe said angrily: "Look! Is any of what you said—well—kidding?"

"I wish it were, fella," said the co-pilot. "I can talk to you about it, but most of it's hushed up. I tell you——"

"Why can you talk to me?" demanded Joe suspiciously. "What makes it all right for you to talk to me?"

"You've got passage on this ship. That means something!"

"Does it?" asked Joe.

The pilot turned in his seat to glance at Joe.

"Do you think we carry passengers regularly?" he asked mildly.

"Why not?"

Pilot and co-pilot looked at each other.

"Tell him," said the pilot.

"About five months ago," said the co-pilot, "there was an Army colonel wangled a ride to Bootstrap on a cargo plane. The plane took off. It flew all right until twenty miles from Bootstrap. Then it stopped checking. It dove straight for the Shed the Platform's being built in. It was shot down. When it hit, there was an explosion." The co-pilot shrugged. "You won't believe me, maybe. But a week later they found the colonel's body back east. Somebody'd murdered him."

Joe blinked.

"It wasn't the colonel who rode as a passenger," said the co-pilot. "It was somebody else. Twenty miles from Bootstrap he'd shot the pilots and taken the controls. That's what they figure, anyhow. He meant to dive into the construction Shed. Because — very, very cleverly — they'd managed to get a bomb in the plane disguised as cargo. They got the men who'd done that, later, but it was rather late."

Joe said dubiously: "But would one bomb destroy the Shed and the Platform?"

"This one would," said the co-pilot. "It was an atom bomb. But it wasn't a good one. It didn't detonate properly. It was a fizz-off."

Joe saw the implications. Cranks and crackpots couldn't get hold of the materials for atom bombs. It took the resources of a large nation for that. But a nation that didn't quite dare start an open war might try to sneak in one atom bomb to destroy the space station. Once the Platform was launched no other nation could dream of world domination. The United States wouldn't go to war if the Platform was destroyed. But there could be a strictly local hot war.

The pilot said sharply: "Something down below!"

The co-pilot fairly leaped into his right-hand seat, his safety belt buckled in half a heartbeat.

"Check," he said in a new tone. "Where?"

The pilot pointed.

"I saw something dark," he said briefly, "where there was a deep dent in the cloud."

The co-pilot threw a switch. Within seconds a new sound entered the cabin. Beep-beep-beep-beep. They were thin squeaks, spaced a full half-second apart, that rose to inaudibility in pitch in the fraction of a second they lasted. The co-pilot snatched a hand phone from the wall above his head and held it to his lips.

"Flight two-twenty calling," he said crisply. "Something's got a radar on us. We saw it. Get a fix on us and come a-running. We're at eighteen thousand and"—here the floor of the cabin tilted markedly—"now we're climbing. Get a fix on us and come a-running. Over!"

He took the phone from his lips and said conversationally: "Radar's a giveaway. This is no fly-way. You wouldn't think he'd take that much of a chance, would you?"

Joe clenched his hands. The pilot did things to the levers on the column between the two pilots' seats. He said curtly: "Arm the jatos."

The co-pilot did something mysterious and said: "Check."

All this took place in seconds. The pilot said, "I see something!" and instantly there was swift, tense teamwork in action. A call by radio, asking for help. The plane headed up for greater clearance between it and the clouds. The jatos made ready for firing. They were the jet-assisted take-off rockets which on a short or rough field would double the motors' thrust for a matter of seconds. In straightaway flight they should make the plane leap ahead like a scared rabbit. But they wouldn't last long.

"I don't like this," said the co-pilot in a flat voice. "I don't see what he could do——"

Then he stopped. Something zoomed out of a cloud. The action was completely improbable. The thing that appeared looked absolutely commonplace. It was a silver-winged private plane, the sort that cruises at one hundred and seventy-five knots and can hit nearly two-fifty if pushed. It was expensive, but not large. It came straight up out of the cloud layer and went lazily over on its back and dived down into the cloud layer again. It looked like somebody

8

stunting for his own private lunatic pleasure—the kind of crazy thing some people do, and for which there is no possible explanation.

But there was an explanation for this.

At the very top of the loop, threads of white smoke appeared. They should have been unnoticeable against the cloud. But for the fraction of an instant they were silhouetted against the silver wings. And they were not misty wisps of vapor. They were dense, sharply defined rocket trails.

They shot upward, spreading out. They unreeled with incredible, ever-increasing velocity.

The pilot hit something with the heel of his hand. There was a heart-stopping delay. Then the transport leaped forward with a force to stop one's breath. The jatos were firing furiously, and the ship jumped. There was a bellowing that drowned out the sound of the engines. Joe was slammed back on the rear wall of the cabin. He struggled against the force that pushed him tailward. He heard the pilot saying calmly: "That plane shot rockets at us. If they're guided we're sunk."

Then the threads of smoke became the thickness of cables, of columns! They should have ringed the transport plane in. But the jatos had jumped it crazily forward and were still thrusting fiercely to make it go faster than any prop-plane could. The acceleration made the muscles at the front of Joe's throat ache as he held his head upright against it.

"They'll be proximity——"

Then the plane bucked. Very probably, at that moment, it was stretched far past the limit of strain for which even its factor of safety was designed. One rocket had let go. The others went with it. The rockets had had proximity fuses. If they had ringed the transport ship and gone off with it enclosed, it would now be a tumbling mass of wreckage. But the jatos had thrown the plane out ahead of the target area. Suddenly they cut off, and it seemed as if the ship had braked. But the pilot dived steeply, for speed.

The co-pilot was saying coldly into the microphone: "He shot rockets. Looked like Army issue three point fives with proximities. They missed. And we're mighty lonely!"

9

The transport tore on, both pilots grimly watching the cloud bank below. They moved their bodies as they stared out the windows, so that by no possibility could any part of the plane mask something that they should see. As they searched, the co-pilot spoke evenly into the microphone at his lips: "He wouldn't carry more than four rockets, and he's dumping his racks and firing equipment now. But he might have a friend with him. Better get here quick if you want to catch him. He'll be the innocentest private pilot you ever saw in no time!"

Then the pilot grunted. Something was streaking across the cloud formation far, far ahead. Three things. They were jet planes, and they seemed not so much to approach as to swell in size. They were coming at better than five hundred knots—ten miles a minute—and the transport was heading for them at its top speed of three hundred knots. The transport and the flight of jets neared each other at the rate of a mile in less than four seconds.

The co-pilot said crisply: "Silver Messner with red wing-tips. The number began——" He gave the letter and first digits of the vanished plane's official designation, without which it could not take off from or be serviced at any flying field.

Joe heard an insistent, swift beep-beep-beep-beep which would be the radars of the approaching jets. He could not hear any answers that might reach the co-pilot as he talked to unseen persons who would relay his words to the jet fighters.

One of them peeled off and sank into the cloud layer. The others came on. They set up in great circles about the transport, crossing before it, above it, around it, which gave the effect of flying around an object not in motion at all.

The pilot flew on, frowning. The co-pilot said: "Yes. Sure! I'm listening!" There was a pause. Then he said: "Check. Thanks."

He hung the instrument back where it belonged, above his head and behind him. He thoughtfully mopped his brow. He looked at Joe.

"Maybe," he said mildly, "you believe me when I tell you there's a sort of hot war on, to keep the Platform from taking off."

The pilot grunted. "Here's the third jet coming up."

It was true. The jet that had dived into the clouds came up out

10

of the cloud formation with somehow an air of impassive satisfaction.

"Did they spot the guy?"

"Yeah," said the co-pilot. "He must've picked up my report. He didn't dump his radar. He stayed in the cloud bank. When the jet came for him—spotting him with its night-fighter stuff—he tried to ram. Tried for a collision. So the jet gave him the works. Blew him apart. Couldn't make him land. Maybe they'll pick up something from the wreckage."

Joe wet his lips.

"I—saw what happened," he said. "He tried to smash us with rockets. Where'd he get them? How were they smuggled in?"

The co-pilot shrugged. "Maybe smuggled in. Maybe stolen. They coulda been landed from a sub anywhere on a good many thousand miles of coast. They coulda been hauled anywhere in a station wagon. The plane was a private-type ship. Plenty of them flying around. It could've been bought easily enough. All they'd need would be a farm somewhere where it could land and they could strap on a rocket rack and put in a radar. And they'd need information. Probably be a good lead, this business. Only just so many people could know what was coming on this ship, and what course it was flying, and so on. Security will have to check back from that angle."

A shadow fell upon the transport ship. A jet shot past from above it. It waggled its wings and changed course.

"We've got to land and be checked for damage," said the co-pilot negligently. "These guys will circle us and lead the way—as if we needed it!"

Joe subsided. He still had in his mind the glamorous and infinitely alluring picture of the Space Platform floating grandly in its orbit, with white-hot sunshine on it and a multitude of stars beyond. He had been completely absorbed in that aspect of the job that dealt with the method of construction and the technical details by which the Platform could be made to work.

Now he had a side light on the sort of thing that has to be done when anything important is achieved. Figuring out how a thing can be done is only part of the job. Overcoming the obstacles to the

11

apparently commonplace steps is nine-tenths of the difficulty. It had seemed to him that the most dramatic aspect of building the Space Platform had been the achievement of a design that would work in space, that could be gotten up into space, and that could be lived in under circumstances never before experienced. Now he saw that getting the materials to the spot where they were needed called for nearly as much brains and effort. Screening out spies and destructionists—that would be an even greater achievement!

He began to feel a tremendous respect and solicitude for the people who were doing ordinary jobs in the building of the Platform. And he worried about his own share more than ever.

Presently the transport ship sank toward the clouds. It sped through them, stone-blind from the mist. And then there was a small airfield below, and the pilot and co-pilot began a pattern of ritualistic conversation.

"Pitot and wing heaters?" asked the pilot.

The co-pilot put his hand successively on two controls.

"Off."

"Spark advance?"

The co-pilot moved his hands.

"Take-off and climb?" said the co-pilot.

"Blowers?"

"Low."

"Fuel selectors?"

The co-pilot moved his hands again to the appropriate controls, verifying that they were as he reported them.

"Main on," he said matter-of-factly, "crossfeed off."

The transport plane slanted down steeply for the landing field that had looked so small at first, but expanded remarkably as they drew near.

Joe found himself frowning. He began to see how really big a job it was to get a Space Platform even ready to take off for a journey that in theory should last forever. It was daunting to think that before a space ship could be built and powered and equipped with machinery there had to be such wildly irrelevant plans worked out as a proper check of controls for the piston-engine ships that flew parts to the job. The details were innumerable!

But the job was still worth doing. Joe was glad he was going to have a share in it.

CHAPTER 2

It was a merely misty day. The transport plane stood by the door of a hangar on this military field, and mechanics stood well back from it and looked it over. A man crawled over the tail assembly and found one small hole in the fabric of the stabilizer. A shell fragment had gone through when the war rockets exploded nearby. The pilot verified that the fragment had hit no strengthening member inside. He nodded. The mechanic made very neat fabric patches over the two holes, upper and lower. He began to go over the fuselage. The pilot turned away.

"I'll go talk to Bootstrap," he told the co-pilot. "You keep an eye on things."

"I'll keep two eyes on them," said the co-pilot.

The pilot went toward the control tower of the field. Joe looked around. The transport ship seemed very large, standing on the concrete apron with its tricycle landing gear let down. It curiously resembled a misshapen insect, standing elaborately high on inadequate supporting legs. Its fuselage, in particular, did not look right for an aircraft. The top of the cargo section went smoothly back to the stabilizing fins, but the bottom did not taper. It ended astern in a clumsy-looking bulge that was closed by a pair of huge clamshell doors, opening straight astern. It was built that way, of course, so that large objects could be loaded direct into the cargo hold, but it was neither streamlined nor graceful.

"Did anything get into the cargo hold?" asked Joe in sudden anxiety. "Did the cases I'm with get hit?"

After all, four rockets had exploded deplorably near the ship. If one fragment had struck, others might have.

"Nothing big, anyhow," the co-pilot told him. "We'll know presently."

But examination showed no other sign of the ship's recent nearness to destruction. It had been overstressed, certainly, but ships are built to take beatings. A spot check on areas where excessive flexing of the wings would have shown up—a big ship's wings are not perfectly rigid: they'd come to pieces in the air if they

14

were—presented no evidence of damage. The ship was ready to take off again.

The co-pilot watched grimly until the one mechanic went back to the side lines. The mechanic was not cordial. He and all the others regarded the ship and Joe and the co-pilot with disfavor. They worked on jets, and to suggest that men who worked on fighter jets were not worthy of complete confidence did not set well with them. The co-pilot noticed it.

"They think I'm a suspicious heel," he said sourly to Joe, "but I have to be. The best spies and saboteurs in the world have been hired to mess up the Platform. When better saboteurs are made, they'll be sent over here to get busy!"

The pilot came back from the control tower.

"Special flight orders," he told his companion. "We top off with fuel and get going."

Mechanics got out the fuel hose, dragging it from the pit. One man climbed up on the wing. Other men handed up the hose. Joe was moved to comment, but the co-pilot was reading the new flight instructions. It was one of those moments of inconsistency to which anybody and everybody is liable. The two men of the ship's crew had it in mind to be infinitely suspicious of anybody examining their ship. But fueling it was so completely standard an operation that they merely stood by absently while it went on. They had the orders to read and memorize, anyhow.

One wing tank was full. A big, grinning man with sandy hair dragged the hose under the nose of the plane to take it to the other wing tank. Close by the nose wheel he slipped and steadied himself by the shaft which reaches down to the wheel's hub. His position for a moment was absurdly ungraceful. When he straightened up, his arm slid into the wheel well. But he dragged the hose the rest of the way and passed it on up. Then that tank was full and capped. The refueling crew got down to the ground and fed the hose back to the pit which devoured it. That was all. But somehow Joe remembered the sandy-haired man and his arm going up inside the wheel well for a fraction of a second.

The pilot read one part of the flight orders again and tore them carefully across. One part he touched his pocket lighter to. It

15

burned. He nodded yet again to the co-pilot, and they swung up and in the pilots' doorway. Joe followed.

They settled in their places in the cabin. The pilot threw a switch and pressed a knob. One motor turned over stiffly, and caught. The second. Third. Fourth. The pilot listened, was satisfied, and pulled back on the multiple throttle. The plane trundled away. Minutes later it faced the long runway, a tinny voice from the control tower spoke out of a loud-speaker under the instruments, and the plane roared down the field. In seconds it lifted and swept around in a great half-circle.

"Okay," said the pilot. "Wheels up."

The co-pilot obeyed. The telltale lights that showed the wheels retracted glowed briefly. The men relaxed.

"You know," said the co-pilot, "there was the devil of a time during the War with sabotage. Down in Brazil there was a field planes used to take off from to fly to Africa. But they'd take off, head out to sea, get a few miles offshore, and then blow up. We must've lost a dozen planes that way! Then it broke. There was a guy—a sergeant—in the maintenance crew who was sticking a hand grenade up in the nose wheel wells. German, he was, and very tidy about it, and nobody suspected him. Everything looked okay and tested okay. But when the ship was well away and the crew pulled up the wheels, that tightened a string and it pulled the pin out of the grenade. It went off.... The master mechanic finally caught him and nearly killed him before the MPs could stop him. We've got to be plenty careful, whether the ground crews like it or not."

Joe said drily: "You were, except when they were topping off. You took that for granted." He told about the sandy-haired man. "He hadn't time to stick anything in the wheel well, though," he added.

The co-pilot blinked. Then he looked annoyed. "Confound it! I didn't watch! Did you?"

The pilot shook his head, his lips compressed.

The co-pilot said bitterly: "And I thought I was security-conscious! Thanks for telling me, fella. No harm done this time, but that was a slip!"

16

He scowled at the dials before him. The plane flew on.

This was the last leg of the trip, and now it should be no more than an hour and a half before they reached their destination. Joe felt a lift of elation. The Space Platform was a realization—or the beginning of it—of a dream that had been Joe's since he was a very small boy. It was also the dream of most other small boys at the time. The Space Platform would make space travel possible. Of course it wouldn't make journeys to the moon or planets itself, but it would sail splendidly about the Earth in an orbit some four thousand miles up, and it would gird the world in four hours fourteen minutes and twenty-two seconds. It would carry atom-headed guided missiles, and every city in the world would be defenseless against it. Nobody could even hope for world domination so long as it floated on its celestial round. Which, naturally, was why there were such desperate efforts to destroy it before its completion.

But Joe, thinking about the Platform, did not think about it as a weapon. It was the first rung on the stepladder to the stars. From it the moon would be reached, certainly. Mars next, most likely. Then Venus. In time the moons of Saturn, and the twilight zone of Mercury, and some day the moons of Jupiter. Possibly a landing could be dared on that giant planet itself, despite its gravity.

The co-pilot spoke suddenly. "How do you rate this trip by cargo plane?" he asked curiously. "Mostly even generals have to go on the ground. You rate plenty. How?"

Joe pulled his thoughts back from satisfied imagining. It hadn't occurred to him that it was remarkable that he should be allowed to accompany the gyros from the plant to their destination. His family firm had built them, so it had seemed natural to him. He wasn't used to the idea that everybody looked suspicious to a security officer concerned with the safety of the Platform.

"Connections? I haven't any," said Joe. Then he said, "I do know somebody on the job. There's a Major Holt out there. He might have cleared me. Known my family for years."

"Yeah," said the co-pilot drily. "He might. As a matter of fact, he's the senior security officer for the whole job. He's in charge of everything, from the security guards to the radar screens and the

17

jet-plane umbrella and the checking of the men who work in the Shed. If he says you're all right, you probably are."

Joe hadn't meant to seem impressive. He explained: "I don't know him too well. He knows my father, and his daughter Sally's been kicking around underfoot most of my life. I taught her how to shoot, and she's a better shot than I am. She was a nice kid when she was little. I got to like her when she fell out of a tree and broke her arm and didn't even whimper. That shows how long ago it was!" He grinned. "She was trying to act grown-up last time I saw her."

The co-pilot nodded. There was a brisk chirping sound somewhere. The pilot reached ahead to the course-correction knob. The plane changed course. Sunshine shifted as it poured into the cabin. The ship was running on automatic pilot well above the cloud level, and at an even-numbered number of thousands of feet altitude, as was suitable for planes traveling south or west. Now it droned on its new course, forty-five degrees from the original. Joe found himself guessing that one of the security provisions for planes approaching the Platform might be that they should not come too near on a direct line to it, lest they give information to curious persons on the ground.

Time went on. Joe slipped gradually back to his meditations about the Platform. There was always, in his mind, the picture of a man-made thing shining in blinding sunlight between Earth and moon. But he began to remember things he hadn't paid too much attention to before.

Opposition to the bare idea of a Space Platform, for instance, from the moment it was first proposed. Every dictator protested bitterly. Even politicians out of office found it a subject for rabble-rousing harangues. The nationalistic political parties, the peddlers of hate, the entrepreneurs of discord—every crank in the world had something to say against the Platform from the first. When they did not roundly denounce it as impious, they raved that it was a scheme by which the United States would put itself in position to rule all the Earth. As a matter of fact, the United States had first proposed it as a United Nations enterprise, so that denunciations that politicians found good politics actually made very poor sense.

18

But it did not get past the General Assembly. The proposal was so rabidly attacked on every side that it was not even passed up to the Council—where it would certainly have been vetoed anyhow.

But it was exactly that furious denunciation which put the Platform through the United States Congress, which had to find the money for its construction.

In Joe's eyes and in the eyes of most of those who hoped for it from the beginning, the Platform's great appeal was that it was the necessary first step toward interplanetary travel, with star ships yet to come. But most scientists wanted it, desperately, for their own ends. There were low-temperature experiments, electronic experiments, weather observations, star-temperature measurements, astronomical observations.... Any man in any field of science could name reasons for it to be built. Even the atom scientists had one, and nearly the best. Their argument was that there were new developments of nuclear theory that needed to be tried out, but should not be tried out on Earth. There were some reactions that ought to yield unlimited power for all the world from really abundant materials. But there was one chance in fifty that they wouldn't be safe, just because the materials were so abundant. No sane man would risk a two-per-cent chance of destroying Earth and all its people, yet those reactions should be tried. In a space ship some millions of miles out in emptiness they could be. Either they'd be safe or they would not. But the only way to get a space ship a safe enough distance from Earth was to make a Space Platform as a starting point. Then a ship could shoot away from Earth with effectively zero gravity and full fuel tanks. The Platform should be built so civilization could surge ahead to new heights!

But despite these excellent reasons, it was the Platform's enemies who really got it built. The American Congress would never have appropriated funds for a Platform for pure scientific research, no matter what peacetime benefits it promised. It was the vehemence of those who hated it that sold it to Congress as a measure for national defense. And in a sense it was.

These were ironic aspects Joe hadn't thought about before, just as he hadn't thought about the need to defend the Platform while it was being built. Defending it was Sally's father's job, and he wouldn't have a popular time. Joe wondered idly how Sally liked living out where the most important job on Earth was being done. She was a nice kid. He remembered appreciatively that she'd grown up to be a very good-looking girl. He tended to remember her mostly as the tomboy who could beat him swimming, but the last time he'd seen her, come to think of it, he'd been startled to observe how pretty she'd grown. He didn't know anybody who ought to be better-looking.... She was a really swell girl....

He came to himself again. There was a change in the look of the sky ahead. There was no actual horizon, of course. There was a white haze that blended imperceptibly into the cloud layer so that it was impossible to tell where the sky ended and the clouds or earth began. But presently there were holes in the clouds. The ship droned on, and suddenly it floated over the edge of such a hole, and looking down was very much like looking over the edge of a cliff at solid earth illimitably far below.

The holes increased in number. Then there were no holes at all, but only clouds breaking up the clear view of the ground beneath. And presently again even the clouds were left behind and the air was clear—but still there was no horizon—and there was brownish earth with small green patches and beyond was sere brown range. At seventeen thousand feet there were simply no details.

Soon the clouds were merely a white-tipped elevation of the white haze to the sides and behind. And then there came a new sound above the droning roar of the motors. Joe heard it—and then he saw.

Something had flashed down from nowhere. It flashed on ahead and banked steeply. It was a fighter jet, and for an instant Joe saw the distant range seem to ripple and dance in its exhaust blast. It circled watchfully.

The transport pilot manipulated something. There was a change in the sound of the motors. Joe followed the co-pilot's eyes. The jet fighter was coming up astern, dive brakes extended to reduce its speed. It overhauled the transport very slowly. And then the transport's pilot touched one of the separate prop-controls gently, and again, and again. Joe, looking at the jet, saw it through the whirling blades. There was an extraordinary stroboscopic effect.

20

One of the two starboard propellers, seen through the other, abruptly took on a look which was not that of mistiness at all, but of writhing, gyrating solidity. The peculiar appearance vanished, and came again, and vanished and appeared yet again before it disappeared completely.

The jet shot on ahead. Its dive brakes retracted. It made a graceful, wallowing, shallow dive, and then climbed almost vertically. It went out of sight.

"Visual check," said the co-pilot drily, to Joe. "We had a signal to give. Individual to this plane. We didn't tell it to you. You couldn't duplicate it."

Joe worked it out painfully. The visual effect of one propeller seen through another—that was identification. It was not a type of signaling an unauthorized or uninformed passenger would expect.

"Also," said the co-pilot, "we have a television camera in the instrument board yonder. We've turned it on now. The interior of the cabin is being watched from the ground. No more tricks like the phony colonel and the atom bomb that didn't 'explode.'"

Joe sat quite still. He noticed that the plane was slanting gradually downward. His eyes went to the dial that showed descent at somewhere between two and three hundred feet a minute. That was for his benefit. The cabin was pressurized, though it did not attempt to simulate sea-level pressure. It was a good deal better than the outside air, however, and yet too quick a descent meant discomfort. Two to three hundred feet per minute is about right.

The ground took on features. Small gulleys. Patches of coloration too small to be seen from farther up. The feeling of speed increased. After long minutes the plane was only a few thousand feet up. The pilot took over manual control from the automatic pilot. He seemed to wait. There was a plaintive, mechanical beep-beep and he changed course.

"You'll see the Shed in a minute or two," said the co-pilot. He added vexedly, as if the thing had been bothering him, "I wish I hadn't missed that sandy-haired guy putting his hand in the wheel well! Nothing happened, but I shouldn't have missed it!"

Joe watched. Very, very far away there were mountains, but he

21

suddenly realized the remarkable flatness of the ground over which they were flying. From the edge of the world, behind, to the very edge of these far-distant hills, the ground was flat. There were gullies and depressions here and there, but no hills. It was flat, flat, flat....

The plane flew on. There was a tiny glimmer of sunlight. Joe strained his eyes. The sunlight glinted from the tiniest possible round pip on the brown earth. It grew as the plane flew on. It was half a cherry stone. It was half an orange, with gores. It was the top section of a sphere that was simply too huge to have been made by men.

There was a thin thread of white that ran across the dun-colored range and reached that half-ball and then ended. It was a highway. Joe realized that the half-globe was the Shed, the monstrous building made for the construction of the Space Platform. It was gigantic. It was colossal. It was the most stupendous thing that men had ever created.

Joe saw a tiny projection near the base of it. It was an office building for clerks and timekeepers and other white-collar workers. He strained his eyes again and saw a motor truck on the highway. It looked extraordinarily flat. Then he saw that it wasn't a single truck but a convoy of them. A long way back, the white highway was marked by a tiny dot. That was a motor bus.

There was no sign of activity anywhere, because the scale was so great. Movement there was, but the things that moved were too small to be seen by comparison with the Shed. The huge, round, shining half-sphere of metal stood tranquilly in the midst of emptiness.

It was bigger than the pyramids.

The plane went on, descending. Joe craned his neck, and then he was ashamed to gawk. He looked ahead, and far away there were white speckles that would be buildings: Bootstrap, the town especially built for the men who built the Space Platform. In it they slept and ate and engaged in the uproarious festivity that men on a construction job crave on their time off.

The plane dipped noticeably.

"Airfield off to the right," said the co-pilot. "That's for the town

22

and the job. The jets—there's an air umbrella overhead all the time—have a field somewhere else. The pushpots have a field of their own, too, where they're training pilots."

Joe didn't know what a pushpot was, but he didn't ask. He was thinking about the Shed, which was the greatest building ever put up, and had been built merely to shelter the greatest hope for the world's peace while it was put together. He'd be in the Shed presently. He'd work there, setting up the contents of the crates back in the cargo space, and finally installing them in the Platform itself.

The pilot said: "Pitot and wing heaters?"

"Off," said the co-pilot.

"Spark and advance——"

Joe didn't listen. He looked down at the sprawling small town with white-painted barracks and a business section and an obvious, carefully designed recreation area that nobody would ever use. The plane was making a great half-circle. The motor noise dimmed as Joe became absorbed in his anticipation of seeing the Space Platform and having a hand in its building.

The co-pilot said sharply: "Hold everything!"

Joe jerked his head around. The co-pilot had his hand on the wheel release. His face was tense.

"It don't feel right," he said very, very quietly. "Maybe I'm crazy, but there was that sandy-haired guy who put his hand up in the wheel well back at that last field. And this don't feel right!"

The plane swept on. The airfield passed below it. The co-pilot very cautiously let go of the wheel release, which when pulled should let the wheels fall down from their wells to lock themselves in landing position. He moved from his seat. His lips were pinched and tight. He scrabbled at a metal plate in the flooring. He lifted it and looked down. A moment later he had a flashlight. Joe saw the edge of a mirror. There were two mirrors down there, in fact. One could look through both of them into the wheel well.

The co-pilot made quite sure. He stood up, leaving the plate off the opening in the floor.

"There's something down in the wheel well," he said in a brittle tone. "It looks to me like a grenade. There's a string tied to it.

23

At a guess, that sandy-haired guy set it up like that saboteur sergeant down in Brazil. Only—it rolled a little. And this one goes off when the wheels go down. I think, too, if we belly-land——Better go around again, huh?"

The pilot nodded. "First," he said evenly, "we get word down to the ground about the sandy-haired guy, so they'll get him regardless."

He picked up the microphone hanging above and behind him and began to speak coldly into it. The transport plane started to swing in wide, sweeping circles over the desert beyond the airport while the pilot explained that there was a grenade in the nose wheel well, set to explode if the wheel were let down or, undoubtedly, if the ship came in to a belly landing.

Joe found himself astonishingly unafraid. But he was filled with a pounding rage. He hated the people who wanted to smash the pilot gyros because they were essential to the Space Platform. He hated them more completely than he had known he could hate anybody. He was so filled with fury that it did not occur to him that in any crash or explosive landing that would ruin the gyros, he would automatically be killed.

CHAPTER 3

The pilot made an examination down the floor-plate hole, with a flashlight to see by and two mirrors to show him the contents of a spot he could not possibly reach with any instrument. Joe heard his report, made to the ground by radio.

"It's a grenade," he said coldly. "It took time to fix it the way it is. At a guess, the ship was booby-trapped at the time of its last overhaul. But it was arranged that the booby trap had to be set, the trigger cocked, by somebody doing something very simple at a different place and later on. We've been flying with that grenade in the wheel well for two weeks. But it was out of sight. Today, back at the airfield, a sandy-haired man reached up and pulled a string he knew how to find. That loosened a slipknot. The grenade rolled down to a new position. Now when the wheel goes down the pin is pulled. You can figure things out from that."

It was an excellent sabotage device. If a ship blew up two weeks after overhaul, it would not be guessed that the bomb had been placed so long before. Every search would be made for a recent opportunity for the bomb's placing. A man who merely reached in and pulled a string that armed the bomb and made it ready for firing would never be suspected. There might be dozens of planes, now carrying their own destruction about with them.

The pilot said into the microphone: "Probably...." He listened. "Very well, sir."

He turned away and nodded to the co-pilot, now savagely keeping the ship in wide, sweeping circles, the rims of which barely touched the farthermost corner of the airport on the ground below.

"We've authority to jump," he said briefly. "You know where the chutes are. But there is a chance I can belly-land without that grenade blowing. I'm going to try that."

The co-pilot said angrily: "I'll get him a chute." He indicated Joe, and said furiously, "They've been known to try two or three tricks, just to make sure. Ask if we should dump cargo before we crash-land!"

The pilot held up the microphone again. He spoke. He listened.

"Okay to dump stuff to lighten ship."

"You won't dump my crates," snapped Joe. "And I'm staying to see you don't! If you can ride this ship down, so can I!"

The co-pilot got up and scowled at him.

"Anything I can move out, goes. Will you help?"

Joe followed him through the door into the cargo compartment.

The space there was very considerable, and bitterly cold. The crates from the Kenmore plant were the heaviest items of cargo. Other objects were smaller. The co-pilot made his way to the rear and pulled a lever. Great, curved doors opened at the back of the plane. Instantly there was such a bellowing of motors that all speech was impossible. The co-pilot pulled out a clip of colored-paper slips and checked one with the nearest movable parcel. He painstakingly made a check mark and began to push the box toward the doors.

It was not a conspicuously sane operation. So near the ground, the plane tended to waver. The air was distinctly bumpy. To push a massive box out a doorway, so it would tumble down a thousand feet to desert sands, was not so safe a matter as would let it become tedious. But Joe helped. They got the box to the door and shoved it out. It went spinning down. The co-pilot hung onto the doorframe and watched it land. He chose another box. He checked it. And another. Joe helped. They got them out of the door and dropping dizzily through emptiness. The plane soared on in circles. The desert, as seen through the opened clamshell doors, reeled away astern, and then seemed to tilt, and reeled away again. Joe and the co-pilot labored furiously. But the co-pilot checked each item before he jettisoned it.

It was a singularly deliberate way to dump cargo to destruction. A metal-bound box. Over the edge of the cargo space floor. A piece of machinery, visible through its crate. A box marked Instruments. Fragile. Each one checked off. Each one dumped to drop a thousand feet or more. A small crated dynamo. This item and that. A crate marked Stationery. It would be printed forms for the timekeepers, perhaps. But it wasn't.

It dropped out. The plane bellowed on. And suddenly there

was a burst of blue-white flame on the desert below. The box that should have contained timecards had contained something very much more explosive. As the plane roared on—rocking from the shock wave of the explosion—Joe saw a crater and a boiling cloud of smoke and flying sand.

The co-pilot spoke explosively and furiously, in the blasting uproar of the motors. He vengefully marked the waybill of the parcel that had exploded. But then they went back to the job of dumping cargo. They worked well as a team now. In no more than minutes everything was out except the four crates that were the gyros. The co-pilot regarded them dourly, and Joe clenched his fists. The co-pilot closed the clamshell doors, and it became possible to hear oneself think again.

"Ship's lighter, anyhow," reported the co-pilot, back in the cabin. "Tell 'em this is what exploded."

The pilot took the slip. He plucked down the microphone—exactly like somebody picking up an interoffice telephone—and reported the waybill number and description of the case that had been an extra bomb. The ship carrying the pilot gyros had been booby-trapped—probably with a number of other ships—and a bomb had been shipped on it, and a special saboteur with a private plane had shot at it with rockets. The pilot gyros were critical devices. They had to be on board the Platform when it took off, and they took months to make and balance. There had been extra pains taken to prevent their arrival!

"I'm dumping gas now," said the pilot into the microphone, "and then coming in for a belly landing."

The ship flew straightaway. It flew more lightly, and it bounced a little. When gas is dumped one has to slow to not more than one hundred and seventy-five knots and fly level. Then one is supposed to fly five minutes after dumping with the chutes in the drain position—and even then there is forty-five minutes of flying fuel still in the tanks.

The ship swept around and headed back for the now far-distant field. It went slowly lower and lower and lower until it seemed barely to skim the minor irregularities in the ground. And low like this, the effect of speed was terrific.

27

The co-pilot thought of something. Quickly he went back into the cargo space. He returned with an armful of blankets. He dumped them on the floor.

"If that grenade does go!" he said sourly.

Joe helped. In the few minutes before Bootstrap loomed near, they filled the bottom of the cabin with blankets. Especially around the pilots' chairs. And there was a mound of blanketing above the actual place where the grenade might be. It made sense. Soft stuff like blankets would absorb an explosion better than anything else. But the pilot thought the grenade might not blow.

"Hold fast!" snapped the pilot.

The wing flaps were down. That slowed the ship a little. It had been lightened. That helped. They went in over the edge of the field less than man-height high. Joe found his hands closing convulsively on a handgrip. He saw a crash wagon starting out from the side of the runway. A fire truck started for the line the plane followed.

Four feet above the rushing sand. Three. The pilot eased back the stick. His face was craggy and very grim and very hard. The ship's tail went down and dragged. It bumped. Then the plane careened and slid and half-whirled crazily, and then the world seemed to come to an end. Crashes. Bangs. Shrieks of torn metal. Bumps, thumps and grindings. Then a roaring.

Joe pulled himself loose from where he had been flung—it seemed to him that he peeled himself loose—and found the pilot struggling up, and he grabbed him to help, and the co-pilot hauled at them both, and abruptly all three of them were in the open air and running at full speed away from the ship.

The roar abruptly became a bellowing. There was an explosion. Flames sprouted everywhere. The three men ran stumblingly. But even as they ran, the co-pilot swore.

"We left something!" he panted.

Joe heard a crescendo of booming, crackling noises behind. Something else exploded dully. But he should be far enough away by now.

He turned to look, and he saw blackening wreckage immersed in roaring flames. The flames were monstrous. They rose sky-high, it seemed—more flames than forty-five minutes of gasoline should have produced. As he looked, something blew up shatteringly, and fire raged even more furiously. Of course in such heat the delicately adjusted gyros would be warped and ruined even if the crash hadn't wrecked them beforehand. Joe made thick, incoherent sounds of rage.

The plane was now an incomplete, twisted skeleton, licked through by flames. The crash wagon roared to a stop beside them.

"Anybody hurt? Anybody left inside?"

Joe shook his head, unable to speak for despairing rage. The fog wagon roared up, already spouting mist from its nozzles. Its tanks contained water treated with detergent so that it broke into the finest of droplets when sprayed at four hundred pounds pressure. It drenched the burning wreck with that heavy mist, in which a man would drown. No fire could possibly sustain itself. In seconds, it seemed, there were only steam and white vapor and fumes of smoldering substances that gradually lessened.

But then there was a roaring of motorcycles racing across the field with a black car trailing them. The car pulled up beside the fog wagon, then sped swiftly to where Joe was coming out of wild rage and sinking into sick, black depression. He'd been responsible for the pilot gyros and their safe arrival. What had happened wasn't his fault, but it was not his job merely to remain blameless. It was his job to get the gyros delivered and set up in the Space Platform. He had failed.

The black car braked to a stop. There was Major Holt. Joe had seen him six months before. He'd aged a good deal. He looked grimly at the two pilots.

"What happened?" he demanded. "You dumped your fuel! What burned like this?"

Joe said thickly: "Everything was dumped but the pilot gyros. They didn't burn! They were packed at the plant!"

The co-pilot suddenly made an incoherent sound of rage. "I've got it!" he said hoarsely. "I know— —"

"What?" snapped Major Holt.

"They—planted that grenade at the—major overhaul!" panted the co-pilot, too enraged even to swear. "They—fixed it so—any trouble would mean a wreck! And I—pulled the fire-extinguisher releases just as we hit! For all compartments! To flood everything with CO2! But it wasn't CO2! That's what burned!"

Major Holt stared sharply at him. He held up his hand. Somebody materialized beside him. He said harshly: "Get the extinguisher bottles sealed and take them to the laboratory."

"Yes, sir!"

A man went running toward the wreck. Major Holt said coldly: "That's a new one. We should have thought of it. You men get yourselves attended to and report to Security at the Shed."

The pilot and co-pilot turned away. Joe turned to go with them. Then he heard Sally's voice, a little bit wobbly: "Joe! Come with us, please!"

Joe hadn't seen her, but she was in the car. She was pale. Her eyes were wide and frightened.

Joe said stiffly: "I'll be all right. I want to look at those crates—"

Major Holt said curtly: "They're already under guard. There'll have to be photographs made before anything can be touched. And I want a report from you, anyhow. Come along!"

Joe looked. The motorcycles were abandoned, and there were already armed guards around the still-steaming wreck, grimly watching the men of the fog wagon as they hunted for remaining sparks or flame. It was noticeable that now nobody moved toward the wreck. There were figures walking back toward the edge of the field. What civilians were about, even to the mechanics on duty, had started out to look at the debris at close range. But the guards were on the job. Nobody could approach. The onlookers went back to their proper places.

"Please, Joe!" said Sally shakily.

Joe got drearily into the car. The instant he seated himself, it was in motion again. It went plunging back across the field and out the entrance. Its horn blared and it went streaking toward the town and abruptly turned to the left. In seconds it was on a broad white highway that left the town behind and led toward the emptiness of the desert.

But not quite emptiness. Far, far away there was a great half-globe rising against the horizon. The car hummed toward it, tires singing. And Joe looked at it and felt ashamed, because this was the

30

home of the Space Platform, and he hadn't brought to it the part for which he alone was responsible.

Sally moistened her lips. She brought out a small box. She opened it. There were bandages and bottles.

"I've a first-aid kit, Joe," she said shakily. "You're burned. Let me fix the worst ones, anyhow!"

Joe looked at himself. One coat sleeve was burned to charcoal. His hair was singed on one side. A trouser leg was burned off around the ankle. When he noticed, his burns hurt.

Major Holt watched her spread a salve on scorched skin. He showed no emotion whatever.

"Tell me what happened," he commanded. "All of it!"

Somehow, there seemed very little to tell, but Joe told it baldly as the car sped on. The great half-ball of metal loomed larger and larger but did not appear to grow nearer as Sally practiced first aid. They came to a convoy of trucks, and the horn blared, and they turned out and passed it. Once they met a convoy of empty vehicles on the way back to Bootstrap. They passed a bus. They went on.

Joe finished drearily: "The pilots did everything anybody could. Even checked off the packages as they were dumped. We reported the one that blew up."

Major Holt said uncompromisingly: "Those were orders. In a sense we've gained something even by this disaster. The pilots are probably right about the plane's having been booby-trapped after its last overhaul, and the traps armed later. I'll have an inspection made immediately, and we'll see if we can find how it was done.

"There's the man you think armed the trap on this plane. An order for his arrest is on the way now. I told my secretary. And— hm.... That CO_2——"

"I didn't understand that," said Joe drearily.

"Planes have CO_2 bottles to put fires out," said the Major impatiently. "A fire in flight lights a red warning light on the instrument panel, telling where it is. The pilot pulls a handle, and CO_2 floods the compartment, putting it out. And this ship was coming in for a crash landing so the pilot—according to orders— flooded all compartments with CO_2. Only it wasn't."

Sally said in horror: "Oh, no!"

31

"The CO2 bottles were filled with an inflammable or an explosive gas," said her father, unbending. "Instead of making a fire impossible, they made it certain. We'll have to watch out for that trick now, too."

Joe was too disheartened for any emotion except a bitter depression and a much more bitter hatred of those who were ready to commit any crime—and had committed most—in the attempt to destroy the Platform.

The Shed that housed it rose and rose against the skyline. It became huge. It became monstrous. It became unbelievable. But Joe could have wept when the car pulled up at an angular, three-story building built out from the Shed's base. From the air, this substantial building had looked like a mere chip. The car stopped. They got out. A sentry saluted as Major Holt led the way inside. Joe and Sally followed.

The Major said curtly to a uniformed man at a desk: "Get some clothes for this man. Get him a long-distance telephone connection to the Kenmore Precision Tool Company. Let him talk. Then bring him to me again."

He disappeared. Sally tried to smile at Joe. She was still quite pale.

"That's Dad, Joe. He means well, but he's not cordial. I was in his office when the report of sabotage to your plane came through. We started for Bootstrap. We were on the way when we saw the first explosion. I—thought it was your ship." She winced a little at the memory. "I knew you were on board. It was—not nice, Joe."

She'd been badly scared. Joe wanted to thump her encouragingly on the back, but he suddenly realized that that would no longer be appropriate. So he said gruffly: "I'm all right."

He followed the uniformed man. He began to get out of his scorched and tattered garments. The sergeant brought him more clothes, and he put them on. He was just changing his personal possessions to the new pockets when the sergeant came back again.

"Kenmore plant on the line, sir."

Joe went to the phone. On the way he discovered that the banging around he'd had when the plane landed had made a number of places on his body hurt.

He talked to his father.

Afterward, he realized that it was a queer conversation. He felt guilty because something had happened to a job that had taken eight months to do and that he alone was escorting to its destination. He told his father about that. But his father didn't seem concerned. Not nearly so much concerned as he should have been. He asked urgent questions about Joe himself. If he was hurt. How much? Where? Joe was astonished that his father seemed to think such matters more important than the pilot gyros. But he answered the questions and explained the exact situation and also a certain desperate hope he was trying to cherish that the gyros might still be repairable. His father gave him advice.

Sally was waiting again when he came out. She took him into her father's office, and introduced him to her father's secretary. Compared to Sally she was an extraordinarily plain woman. She wore a sorrowful expression. But she looked very efficient.

Joe explained carefully that his father said for him to hunt up Chief Bender—working on the job out here—because he was one of the few men who'd left the Kenmore plant to work elsewhere, and he was good. He and the Chief, between them, would estimate the damage and the possibility of repair.

Major Holt listened. He was military and official and harassed and curt and tired. Joe'd known Sally and therefore her father all his life, but the Major wasn't an easy man to be relaxed with. He spoke into thin air, and immediately his sad-seeming secretary wrote out a pass for Joe. Then Major Holt gave crisp orders on a telephone and asked questions, and Sally said: "I know. I'll take him there. I know my way around."

Her father's expression did not change. He simply included Sally in his orders on the phone.

He hung up and said briefly: "The plane will be surveyed and taken apart as soon as possible. By the time you find your man you can probably examine the crates. I'll have you cleared for it."

His secretary reached in a drawer for order forms to fill out and hand him to sign. Sally tugged at Joe's arm. They left.

Outside, she said: "There's no use arguing with my father, Joe. He has a terrible job, and it's on his mind all the time. He hates

33

being a Security officer, too. It's a thankless job—and no Security officer ever gets to be more than a major. His ability never shows. What he does is never noticed unless it fails. So he's frustrated. He's got poor Miss Ross—his secretary, you know—so she just listens to what he says must be done and she writes it out. Sometimes he goes days without speaking to her directly. But really it's pretty bad! It's like a war with no enemy to fight except spies! And the things they do! They've been known even to booby-trap a truck after an accident, so anybody who tries to help will be blown up! So everything has to be done in a certain way or everything will be ruined!"

She led him to an office with a door that opened directly into the Shed. In spite of his bitterness, Joe was morosely impatient to see inside. But Sally had to identify him formally as the Joe Kenmore who was the subject of her father's order, and his fingerprints had to be taken, and somebody had him stand for a moment before an X-ray screen. Then she led him through the door, and he was in the Shed where the Space Platform was under construction.

It was a vast cavern of metal sheathing and spidery girders, filled with sound and detail. It took him seconds to begin to absorb what he saw and heard. The Shed was five hundred feet high in the middle, and it was all clear space without a single column or interruption. There were arc lamps burning about its edges, and high up somewhere there were strips of glass which let in a pale light. All of it resounded with many noises and clanging echoes of them.

There were rivet guns at work, and there were the grumblings of motor trucks moving about, and the oddly harsh roar of welding torches. But the torch flames looked only like marsh fires, blue-white and eerie against the mass of the thing that was being built.

It was not too clear to the eye, this incomplete Space Platform. There seemed to be a sort of mist, a glamour about it, which was partly a veiling mass of scaffolding. But Joe gazed at it with an emotion that blotted out even his aching disappointment and feeling of shame.

It was gigantic. It had the dimensions of an ocean liner. It was strangely shaped. Partly obscured by the fragile-seeming framework about it, there was bright plating in swelling curves, and the plating reached up irregularly and followed a peculiar pattern, and above the plating there were girders—themselves shining brightly in the light of many arc lamps—and they rose up and up toward the roof of the Shed itself. The Platform was ungainly and it was huge, and it rested under a hollow metal half-globe that could have doubled for a sky. It was more than three hundred feet high, itself, and there were men working on the bare bright beams of its uppermost parts—and the men were specks. The far side of the Shed's floor had other men on it, and they were merely jerkily moving motes. You couldn't see their legs as they walked. The Shed and the Platform were monstrous!

Joe felt Sally's eyes upon him. Somehow, they looked proud. He took a deep breath.

She said: "Come on."

They walked across acres of floor neatly paved with shining wooden blocks. They moved toward the thing that was to take mankind's first step toward the stars. As they walked centerward, a big sixteen-wheel truck-and-trailer outfit backed out of an opening under the lacy haze of scaffolds. It turned clumsily, and carefully circled the scaffolding, and moved toward a sidewall of the Shed. A section of the wall—it seemed as small as a rabbit hole—lifted inward like a flap, and the sixteen-wheeler trundled out into the blazing sunlight. Four other trucks scurried out after it. Other trucks came in. The sidewall section closed.

There was the smell of engine fumes and hot metal and of ozone from electric sparks. There was that indescribable smell a man can get homesick for, of metal being worked by men. Joe walked like someone in a dream, with Sally satisfiedly silent beside him, until the scaffolds—which had looked like veiling—became latticework and he saw openings.

They walked into one such tunnel. The bulk of the Platform above them loomed overhead with a crushing menace. There were trucks rumbling all around underneath, here in this maze of scaffold columns. Some carried ready-loaded cages waiting to be snatched up by hoists. Crane grips came down, and snapped fast on the cages, and lifted them up and up and out of sight. There was a Diesel running somewhere, and a man stood and stared skyward and made motions with his hands, and the Diesel adjusted its running to his signals. Then some empty cages came down and landed in a waiting truck body with loud clanking noises. Somebody cast off the hooks, and the truck grumbled and drove away.

Sally spoke to a preoccupied man in shirt sleeves with a badge on an arm band near his shoulder. He looked carefully at the passes she carried, using a flashlight to make sure. Then he led them to a shaft up which a hoist ran. It was very noisy here. A rivet gun banged away overhead, and the plates of the Platform rang with the sound, and the echoes screeched, and to Joe the bedlam was infinitely good to hear. The man with the arm band shouted into a telephone transmitter, and a hoist cage came down. Joe and Sally stepped on it. Joe took a firm grip on her shoulder, and the hoist shot upward.

The hugeness of the Shed and the Platform grew even more apparent as the hoist accelerated toward the roof. The flooring seemed to expand. Spidery scaffold beams dropped past them. There were things being built over by the sidewall. Joe saw a crawling in-plant tow truck moving past those enigmatic objects. It was a tiny truck, no more than four feet high and with twelve-inch wheels. It dragged behind it flat plates of metal with upturned forward edges. They slid over the floor like sledges. Cryptic loads were carried on those plates, and the tow truck stopped by a mass of steel piping being put together, and began to unload the plates.

Then the hoist slowed abruptly and Sally winced a little. The hoist stopped.

Here—two hundred feet up—a welding crew worked on the skin of the Platform itself. The plating curved in and there was a wide flat space parallel to the ground. There was also a great gaping hole beyond. Though girders rose roofward even yet, this was as high as the plating had gone. That opening—Joe guessed— would ultimately be the door of an air lock, and this flat surface was designed for a tender rocket to anchor to by magnets. When a rocket came up from Earth with supplies or reliefs for the

36

Platform's crew, or with fuel to be stored for an exploring ship's later use, it would anchor here and then inch toward that doorway....

There were half a dozen men in the welding crew. They should have been working. But two men battered savagely at each other, their tools thrown down. One was tall and lean, with a wrinkled face and an expression of intolerable fury. The other was squat and dark with a look of desperation. A third man was in the act of putting down his welding torch—he'd carefully turned it off first—to try to interfere. Another man gaped. Still another was climbing up by a ladder from the scaffold level below.

Joe put Sally's hand on the hoist upright, instinctively freeing himself for action.

The lanky man lashed out a terrific roundhouse blow. It landed, but the stocky man bored in. Joe had an instant's clear sight of his face. It was not the face of a man enraged. It had the look of a man both desperate and despairing.

Then the lanky man's foot slipped. He lost balance, and the stocky man's fist landed. The thin man reeled backward. Sally cried out, choking. The lanky man teetered on the edge of the flat place. Behind him, the plating curved down. Below him there were two hundred feet of fall through the steel-pipe maze of scaffolds. If he took one step back he was gone inexorably down a slope on which he could never stop.

He took that step. The stocky man's face abruptly froze in horror. The lanky man stiffened convulsively. He couldn't stop. He knew it. He'd go back and on over the rounded edge, and fall. He might touch the scaffolding. It would not stop him. It would merely set his body spinning crazily as it dropped and crashed again and again before it landed two hundred feet below.

It was horror in slow motion, watching the lean man stagger backward to his death.

Then Joe leaped.

37

CHAPTER 4

For an instant, in mid-air, Joe was incongruously aware of all the noises in the Shed. The murky, girdered ceiling still three hundred feet above him. The swelling, curving, glittering surface of steel underneath. Then he struck. He landed beside the lean man, with his left arm outstretched to share his impetus with him. Alone, he would have had momentum enough to carry himself up the slope down which the man had begun to descend. But now he shared it. The two of them toppled forward together. Their arms were upon the flat surface, while their bodies dangled. The feel of gravity pulling them slantwise and downward was purest nightmare.

But then, as Joe's innards crawled, the same stocky man who had knocked the lean man back was dragging frantically at both of them to pull them to safety.

Then there were two men pulling. The stocky man's face was gray. His horror was proof that he hadn't intended murder. The man who'd put down his welding torch pulled. The man who'd been climbing the ladder put his weight to the task of getting them back to usable footing. They reached safety. Joe scrambled to his feet, but he felt sick at the pit of his stomach. The stocky man began to shake horribly. The lanky one advanced furiously upon him.

"I didn' mean to keel you, Haney!" the dark one panted.

The lanky one snapped: "Okay. You didn't. But come on, now! We finish this——"

He advanced toward the workman who had so nearly caused his death. But the other man dropped his arms to his sides.

"I don' fight no more," he said thickly. "Not here. You keel me is okay. I don' fight."

The lanky man—Haney—growled at him.

"Tonight, then, in Bootstrap. Now get back to work!"

The stocky man picked up his tools. He was trembling.

Haney turned to Joe and said ungraciously: "Much obliged. What's up?"

Joe still felt queasy. There is rarely any high elation after one

38

has risked his life for somebody else. He'd nearly plunged two hundred feet to the floor of the Shed with Haney. But he swallowed.

"I'm looking for Chief Bender. You're Haney? Foreman?"

"Gang boss," said Haney. He looked at Joe and then at Sally who was holding convulsively to the upright Joe had put her hand on. Her eyes were closed. "Yeah," said Haney. "The Chief took off today. Some kind of Injun stuff. Funeral, maybe. Want me to tell him something? I'll see him when I go off shift."

There was an obscure movement somewhere on this part of the Platform. A tiny figure came out of a crevice that would someday be an air lock. Joe didn't move his eyes toward it. He said awkwardly: "Just tell him Joe Kenmore's in town and needs him. He'll remember me, I think. I'll hunt him up tonight."

"Okay," said Haney.

Joe's eyes went to the tiny figure that had come out from behind the plating. It was a midget in baggy, stained work garments like the rest of the men up here. He wore a miniature welding shield pushed back on his head. Joe could guess his function, of course. There'd be corners a normal-sized man couldn't get into, to buck a rivet or weld a joint. There'd be places only a tiny man could properly inspect. The midget regarded Joe without expression.

Joe turned to the hoist to go down to the floor again. Haney waved his hand. The midget lifted his, in grave salutation.

The hoist dropped down the shaft. Sally opened her eyes.

"You—saved that man's life, Joe," she said unsteadily. "But you scared me to death!"

Joe tried to ignore the remark, but he still seemed to feel slanting metal under him and a drop of two hundred feet below. It had been a nightmarish sensation.

"I didn't think," he said uncomfortably. "It was a crazy thing to do. Lucky it worked out."

Sally glanced at him. The hoist still dropped swiftly. Levels of scaffolding shot upward past them. If Joe had slipped down that rolling curve of metal, he'd have dropped past all these. It was not good to think about. He swallowed again. Then the hoist checked in

39

its descent. It stopped. Joe somewhat absurdly helped Sally off to solid ground.

"It—looks to me," said Sally, "as if you're bound to make me see somebody killed. Joe, would you mind leading a little bit less adventurous life for a while? While I'm around?"

He managed to grin. But he still did not feel right.

"Nothing I can do until I can look at the plane," he said, changing the subject, "and I can't find the Chief until tonight. Could we sightsee a little?"

She nodded. They went out from under the intricate framework that upheld the Platform. They went, in fact, completely under that colossal incomplete object. Sally indicated the sidewall.

"Let's go look at the pushpots. They're fascinating!"

She led the way. The enormous spaciousness of the Shed again became evident. There was a catwalk part way up the inward curving wall. Someone leaned on its railing and surveyed the interior of the Shed. He would probably be a security man. Maybe the fist fight up on the Platform had been seen, or maybe not. The man on the catwalk was hardly more than a speck, and it occurred to Joe that there must be other watchers' posts high up on the outer shell where men could search the sunlit desert outside for signs of danger.

But he turned and looked yearningly back at the monstrous thing under the mist of scaffolding. For the first time he could make out its shape. It was something like an egg, but a great deal more like something he couldn't put a name to. Actually it was exactly like nothing in the world but itself, and when it was out in space there would be nothing left on Earth like it.

It would be in a fashion a world in itself, independent of the Earth that made it. There would be hydroponic tanks in which plants would grow to purify its air and feed its crew. There would be telescopes with which men would be able to study the stars as they had never been able to do from the bottom of Earth's ocean of turbulent air. But it would serve Earth.

There would be communicators. They would pick up microwave messages and retransmit them to destinations far around the curve of the planet, or else store them and retransmit them to the other side of the world an hour or two hours later.

It would store fuel with which men could presently set out for the stars—and out to emptiness for nuclear experiments that must not be made on Earth. And finally it would be armed with squat, deadly atomic missiles that no nation could possibly defy. And so this Space Platform would keep peace on Earth.

But it could not make good will among men.

Sally walked on. They reached the mysterious objects being manufactured in a row around half the sidewall of the Shed. They were of simple design and, by comparison, not unduly large. The first objects were merely frameworks of metal pipe, which men were welding together unbreakably. They were no bigger than— say—half of a six-room house. A little way on, these were filled with intricate arrays of tanks and piping, and still farther—there was a truck and hoist unloading a massive object into place right now—there were huge engines fitting precisely into openings designed to hold them. Others were being plated in with metallic skins.

At the very end of this assembly line a crane was loading a finished object onto a flat-bed trailer. As it swung in the air, Joe realized what it was. It might be called a jet plane, but it was not of any type ever before used. More than anything else, it looked like a beetle. It would not be really useful for anything but its function at the end of Operation Stepladder. Then hundreds of these ungainly objects would cluster upon the Platform's sides, like swarming bees. They would thrust savagely up with their separate jet engines. They would lift the Platform from the foundation on which it had been built. Tugging, straining, panting, they would get it out of the Shed. But their work would not end there. Holding it aloft, they would start it eastward, lifting effortfully. They would carry it as far and as high and as fast as their straining engines could work. Then there would be one last surge of fierce thrusting with oversize jato rockets, built separately into each pushpot, all firing at once.

Finally the clumsy things would drop off and come bumbling back home, while the Platform's own rockets flared out their mile-long flames—and it headed up for emptiness.

41

But the making of these pushpots and all the other multitudinous activities of the Shed would have no meaning if the contents of four crates in the wreckage of a burned-out plane could not be salvaged and put to use again.

Joe said restlessly: "I want to see all this, Sally, and maybe anything else I do is useless, but I've got to find out what happened to the gyros I was bringing here!"

Sally said nothing. She turned, and they moved across the long, long space of wood-block flooring toward the doorway by which they had entered. And now that he had seen the Space Platform, all of Joe's feeling of guilt and despondency came back. It seemed unbearable. They went out through the guarded door, Sally surrendered the pass, and Joe was again checked carefully before he was free to go.

Then Sally said: "You don't want me tagging around, do you?"

Joe said honestly: "It isn't exactly that, Sally, but if the stuff is really smashed, I'd—rather not have anybody see me. Please don't be angry, but—"

Sally said quietly: "I know. I'll get somebody to drive you over."

She vanished. She came back with the uniformed man who'd driven Major Holt. She put her hand momentarily on Joe's arm.

"If it's really bad, Joe, tell me. You won't let yourself cry, but I'll cry for you." She searched his eyes. "Really, Joe!"

He grinned feebly and went out to the car.

The feeling on the way to the airfield was not a good one. It was twenty-odd miles from the Shed, but Joe dreaded what he was going to see. The black car burned up the road. It turned to the right off the white highway, onto the curved short cut—and there was the field.

And there was the wreck of the transport plane, still where it had crashed and burned. There were still armed guards about it, but men were working on the wreck, cutting it apart with torches. Already some of it was dissected.

Joe went to the remains of the four crates.

The largest was bent askew by the force of the crash or an

explosion, Joe didn't know which. The smallest was a twisted mass of charcoal. Joe gulped, and dug into them with borrowed tools.

The pilot gyros of the Space Platform would apply the torque that would make the main gyros shift it to any desired position, or else hold it absolutely still. They were to act, in a sense, as a sort of steering engine on the take-off and keep a useful function out in space. If a star photograph was to be made, it was essential that the Platform hold absolutely still while the exposure lasted. If a guided missile was to be launched, it must be started right, and the pilot gyros were needed. To turn to receive an arriving rocket from Earth....

The pilot gyros were the steering apparatus of the Space Platform. They had to be more than adequate. They had to be perfect! On the take-off alone, they were starkly necessary. The Platform couldn't hope to reach its orbit without them.

Joe chipped away charred planks. He pulled off flame-eaten timbers. He peeled off carbonized wrappings—but some did not need to be peeled: they crumbled at a touch—and in twenty minutes he knew the whole story. The rotor motors were ruined. The couplers—pilot-to-main-gyro connections—had been heated red hot and were no longer hardened steel; their dimensions had changed and they would no longer fit. But these were not disastrous items. They were serious, but not tragic.

The tragedy was the gyros themselves. On their absolute precision and utterly perfect balance the whole working of the Platform would depend. And the rotors were gashed in one place, and the shafts were bent. Being bent and nicked, the precision of the apparatus was destroyed. Its precision lost, the whole device was useless. And it had taken four months' work merely to get it perfectly balanced!

It had been the most accurate piece of machine work ever done on Earth. It was balanced to a microgram—to a millionth of the combined weight of three aspirin tablets. It would revolve at 40,000 revolutions per minute. It had to balance perfectly or it would vibrate intolerably. If it vibrated at all it would shake itself to pieces, or, failing that, send aging sound waves through all the Platform's substance. If it vibrated by the least fraction of a ten-

43

thousandth of an inch, it would wear, and vibrate more strongly, and destroy itself and possibly the Platform. It needed the precision of an astronomical telescope's lenses—multiplied! And it was bent. It was exactly as useless as if it had never been made at all.

Joe felt as a man might feel if the mirror of the greatest telescope on earth, in his care, had been smashed. As if the most priceless picture in the world, in his charge, had been burned. But he felt worse. Whether it was his fault or not—and it wasn't—it was destroyed.

A truck rolled up and was stopped by a guard. There was talk, and the guard let it through. A small crane lift came over from the hangars. Its normal use was the lifting of plane motors in and out of their nacelles. Now it was to pick up the useless pieces of equipment on which the best workmen and the best brains of the Kenmore Precision Tool Company had worked unceasingly for eight calendar months, and which now was junk.

Joe watched, numbed by disaster, while the crane hook went down to position above the once-precious objects. Men shored up the heavy things and ran planks under them, and then deftly fitted rope slings for them to be lifted by. It was late afternoon by now. Long shadows were slanting as the crane truck's gears whined, and the slack took up, and the first of the four charred objects lifted and swung, spinning slowly, to the truck that had come from the Shed.

Joe froze, watching. He watched the second. The third did not spin. It merely swayed. But the fourth.... The lines up to the crane hook were twisted. As the largest of the four crates lifted from its bed, it twisted the lines toward straightness. It spun. It spun more and more rapidly, and then more and more slowly, and stopped, and began to spin back.

Then Joe caught his breath. It seemed that he hadn't breathed in minutes. The big crate wasn't balanced. It was spinning. It wasn't vibrating. It spun around its own center of gravity, unerringly revealed by its flexible suspension.

He watched until it was dropped into the truck. Then he went stiffly over to the driver of the car that had brought him.

"Everything's all right," he said, feeling a queer astonishment at his own words. "I'm going to ride back to the Shed with the stuff

44

I brought. It's not hurt too much. I'll be able to fix it with a man or two I can pick up out here. But I don't want anything else to happen to it!"

So he rode back out to the Shed on the tailboard of the truck that carried the crates. The sun set as he rode. He was smudged and disheveled. The reek of charred wood and burnt insulation and scorched wrappings was strong in his nostrils. But he felt very much inclined to sing.

It occurred to Joe that he should have sent Sally a message that she didn't need to cry as a substitute for him. He felt swell! He knew how to do the job that would let the Space Platform take off! He'd tell her, first chance.

It was very good to be alive.

CHAPTER 5

There was nobody in the world to whom the Space Platform was meaningless. To Joe and a great many people like him, it was a dream long and stubbornly held to and now doggedly being made a reality. To some it was the prospect of peace and the hope of a quiet life: children and grandchildren and a serene look forward to the future. Some people prayed yearningly for its success, though they could have no other share in its making. And of course there were those men who had gotten into power and could not stay there without ruthlessness. They knew what the Platform would mean to their kind. For, once world peace was certain, they would be killed by the people they ruled over. So they sent grubby, desperate men to wreck it at any cost. They were prepared to pay for or to commit any crime if the Space Platform could be smashed and turmoil kept as the norm of life on Earth.

And there were the people who were actually doing the building.

Joe rode a bus into Bootstrap that night with some of them. The middle shift—two to ten o'clock—was off. Fleets of busses rolled out from the small town twenty miles away, their headlights making a procession of paired flames in the darkness. They rolled into the unloading area and disgorged the late shift—ten to six—to be processed by security and admitted to the Shed. Then, quite empty, the busses went trundling around to where Joe waited with the released shift milling around him.

The busses stopped and opened their doors. The waiting men stormed in, shoving zestfully, calling to each other, scrambling for seats or merely letting themselves be pushed on board. The bus Joe found himself on was jammed in seconds. He held on to a strap and didn't notice. He was absorbed in the rapt contemplation of his idea for the repair of the pilot gyros. The motors could be replaced easily enough. The foundation of his first despair had been the belief that everything could be managed but one thing; that the all-important absolute accuracy was the only thing that couldn't be achieved. Getting that accuracy, back at the plant, had consumed four months of time. Each of the gyros was four feet in diameter and weighed five hundred pounds. Each spun at 40,000 r.p.m. It had to be machined from a special steel to assure that it would not fly to pieces from sheer centrifugal force. Each was plated with iridium lest a speck of rust form and throw it off balance. If the shaft and bearings were not centered exactly at the center of gravity of the rotors—five hundred pounds of steel off balance at 40,000 r.p.m. could raise the devil. They could literally wreck the Platform itself. And "exactly at the center of gravity" meant exactly. There could be no error by which the shaft was off center by the thousandth of an inch, or a ten-thousandth, or even the tenth of a ten-thousandth. The accuracy had to be absolute.

Gloating over the solution he'd found, Joe could have hugged himself. Hanging to a strap in the waiting bus, he saw another bus start off with a grinding of gears and a spouting of exhaust smoke. It trundled to the highway and rolled away. Another and another followed it. Joe's bus fell in line. They headed for Bootstrap in a convoy, a long, long string of lighted vehicles running one behind the other.

It was dark outside. The Shed was alone, for security. It was twenty miles from the town where its work force slept and ate and made merry. That was security too. One shift came off, and went through a security check, and during that time the Shed was empty save for the security officers who roamed it endlessly, looking for trouble. Sometimes they found it. The shift coming on also passed through a security check. Nobody could get into the Shed without being identified past question. The picture-badge stage was long since passed on the Space Platform job. Security was tight!

The long procession of busses rolled through the night. Outside was dark desert. Overhead were many stars. Inside the jammed bus were swaying figures crowded in the aisle, and every seat was filled. There was the smell of sweat, and oil, and tobacco. Somebody still had garlic on his breath from lunch. There was the noise of many voices. There was an argument two seats up the aisle. There was the rumble of the motor, and the peculiar whine of spinning tires. Men had to raise their voices to be heard above the din.

47

A swaying among the crowded figures more pronounced than that caused by the motion of the bus caught Joe's eye. Somebody was crowding his way from the back toward the front. The aisle was narrow. Joe clung to his strap, thinking hard and happily about the rebalancing of the gyros. There could be no tolerance. It had to be exact. There had to be no vibration at all....

Figures swayed away from him. A hand on his shoulder.

"Hiya."

He swung around. It was the lean man, Haney, whom he'd kept from being knocked off the level place two hundred feet up.

Joe said: "Hello."

"I thought you were big brass," said Haney, rumbling in his ear. "But big brass don't ride the busses."

"I'm going in to try to hunt up the Chief," said Joe.

Haney grunted. He looked estimatingly at Joe. His glance fell to Joe's hands. Joe had been digging further into the crates, and afterward he'd washed up, but packing grease is hard to get off. When mixed with soot and charcoal it leaves signs. Haney relaxed.

"We mostly eat together," he observed, satisfied that Joe was regular because his hands weren't soft and because mechanic's soap had done an incomplete job on them. "The Chief's a good guy. Join us?"

"Sure!" said Joe. "And thanks."

A brittle voice sounded somewhere around Haney's knees. Joe looked down, startled. The midget he'd seen up on the Platform nodded up at him. He'd squirmed through the press in Haney's wake. He seemed to bristle a little out of pure habit. Joe made room for him.

"I'm okay," said the midget pugnaciously.

Haney made a formal introduction.

"Mike Scandia." He thumbed at Joe. "Joe Kenmore. He's eating with us. Wants to find the Chief."

There had been no reference to the risk Joe had run in keeping Haney from a two-hundred-foot fall. But now Haney said approvingly: "I wanted to say thanks anyhow for keeping your mouth shut. New here?"

48

Joe nodded. The noise in the bus made any sort of talk difficult. Haney appeared used to it.

"Saw you with—uh—Major Holt's daughter," he observed again. "That's why I thought you were brass. Figured one or the other'd tell on Braun. You didn't, or somebody'd've raised Cain. But I'll handle it."

Braun would be the man Haney had been fighting. If Haney wanted to handle it his way, it was naturally none of Joe's business. He said nothing.

"Braun's a good guy," said Haney. "Crazy, that's all. He picked that fight. Picked it! Up there! Coulda been him knocked off—and I'd ha' been in a mess! I'll see him tonight."

The midget said something biting in his peculiarly cracked and brittle voice.

The bus rolled and rolled and rolled. It was a long twenty miles to Bootstrap. The desert outside the bus windows was utterly black and featureless, but once a convoy of trucks passed, going to the Shed.

Presently, though, lights twinkled in the night. Again the bus slowed, in column with the others. Then there were barrackslike buildings, succeeding each other, and then there was a corner and suddenly the outside was ablaze with light. The busses drew up to the curb and stopped, and everybody was immediately in a great hurry to get out, shoving unnecessarily, and Joe let himself be carried along by the crowd.

He found himself on the sidewalk with bright neon signs up and down the street. He was in the midst of the crowd which was the middle shift released. It eddied and dispersed without seeming to lessen. Most of the figures in sight were men. There were very, very few women. The neon signs proclaimed that here one could buy beer, and that this was Fred's Place, and that was Sid's Steak Joint. Bowling. Pool. A store—still open for this shift's trade—sold fancy shirts and strictly practical work clothes and highly eccentric items of personal adornment. A movie house. A second. A third. Somewhere a record shop fed repetitious music to the night air. There was movement and crowding and jostling, but the middle of the street was almost empty save for the busses. There were some

49

bicycles, but practically no other wheeled traffic. After all, Bootstrap was strictly a security town. A man could leave whenever he chose, but there were formalities, and personal cars weren't practical.

"Chief'll be yonder," said Haney in Joe's ear. "Come along."

They shouldered their way along the sidewalk. The passers-by were of a type—construction men. Somebody here had taken part in the building of every skyscraper and bridge and dam put up in Joe's lifetime. They could have been kept away from the Space Platform job only by a flat refusal by security to let them be hired.

Haney and Joe moved toward Sid's Steak Joint, with Mike the midget marching truculently between them. Men nodded to them as they passed. Joe marshaled in his mind what he was going to tell the Chief. He had a trick for fixing the pilot gyros. A speck of rust would spoil them, and they had been through a plane crash and a fire and explosions, but his trick would do, in ten days or less, what the plant back home had needed four months to accomplish. The trick was something to gloat over.

Into Sid's Steak Joint. A juke box was playing. Over in a booth, four men ate hungrily, with a slot TV machine in the wall beside them showing wrestling matches out in San Francisco. A waiter carried a huge tray from which steam and fragrant odors arose.

There was the Chief, dark and saturnine to look at, with his straight black hair gleaming in the light. He was a Mohawk, and he and his tribe had taken to steel construction work a long time back. They were good. There were not many big construction jobs on which the Chief's tribesmen were not to be found working. Forty of them had died together in the worst construction accident in history, when a bridge on its way to completion collapsed in the making, but there were a dozen or more at work on the Space Platform now. The Chief had essayed machine-tool work at the Kenmore plant, and he'd been good. He'd pitched on the plant baseball team, and he'd sung bass in the church choir, but there had been nobody else around who talked Indian, and he'd gotten lonely. At that, though, he'd left because the Space Platform began and wild horses couldn't have kept him away from a job like that!

He'd held a table for Haney and Mike, but his eyes widened

50

when he saw Joe. Then he grinned and almost upset the table to stand up and greet him.

"Son-of-a-gun!" he said warmly. "What you doin' here?"

"Right now," said Joe. "I'm looking for you. I've got a job for you."

The Chief, still grinning, shook his head.

"Not me, I'm here till the Platform's done."

"It's on the job," said Joe. "I've got to get a crew together to repair something I brought out here today and that got smashed in the landing."

The four of them sat down. Mike's chin was barely above the table top. The Chief waved to a waiter. "Steaks all around!" he bellowed. Then he bent toward Joe. "Shoot it!"

Joe told his story. Concisely. The pilot gyros, which had to be perfect, had been especially gunned at by saboteurs. An attack with possibly stolen proximity-fused rockets. The plane was booby-trapped, and somebody at an airfield had had a chance to spring the trap. So it was wreckage. Crashed and burned on landing.

The Chief growled. Haney pressed his lips together. The eyes of Mike were burning.

"Plenty of that sabotage stuff," growled the Chief. "Hard to catch the so-and-sos. Smash the gyros and the take-off'd have to wait till new ones got made—and that's more time for more sabotage."

Joe said carefully: "I think it can be licked. Listen a minute, will you?"

The Chief fixed his eyes upon him.

"The gyros have to be rebalanced," said Joe. "They have to spin on their own center of gravity. At the plant, they set them up, spun them, and found which side was heavy. They took metal off till it ran smoothly at five hundred r.p.m. Then they spun it at a thousand. It vibrated. They found imbalance that was too small to show up before. They fixed that. They speeded it up. And so on. They tried to make the center of gravity the center of the shaft by trimming off the weight that put the center of gravity somewhere else. Right?"

The Chief said irritably: "No other way to do it! No other way!"

51

"I saw one," said Joe. "When they cleaned up the wreck at the airfield, they heaved up the crates with a crane. The slings were twisted. Every crate spun as it rose. But not one wobbled! They found their own centers of gravity and spun around them!"

The Chief scowled, deep in thought. Then his face went blank.

"By the holy mud turtle!" he grunted. "I get it!"

Joe said, with very great pains not to seem triumphant, "Instead of spinning the shaft and trimming the rotor, we'll spin the rotor and trim the shaft. We'll form the shaft around the center of gravity, instead of trying to move the center of gravity to the middle of the shaft. We'll spin the rotors on a flexible bearing base. I think it'll work."

Surprisingly, it was Mike the midget who said warmly, "You got it! Yes, sir, you got it!"

The Chief took a deep breath. "Yeah! And d'you know how I know? The Plant built a high-speed centrifuge once. Remember?" He grinned with the triumph Joe concealed. "It was just a plate with a shaft in the middle. There were vanes on the plate. It fitted in a shaft hole that was much too big. They blew compressed air up the shaft hole. It floated the plate up, the air hit the vanes and spun the plate—and it ran as sweet as honey! Balanced itself and didn't wobble a bit! We'll do something like that! Sure!"

"Will you work on it with me?" asked Joe. "We'll need a sort of crew—three or four altogether. Have to figure out the stuff we need. I can ask for anybody I want. I'm asking for you. You pick the others."

The Chief grinned broadly. "Any objections, Haney? You and Mike and me and Joe here? Look!"

He pulled a pencil out of his pocket. He started to draw on the plastic table top, and then took a paper napkin instead.

"Something like this——"

The steaks came, sizzling on the platters they'd been cooked in. The outside was seared, and the inside was hot and deliciously rare. Intellectual exercises like the designing of a machine-tool operation could not compete with such aromas and sights and sounds. The four of them fell to.

But they talked as they ate. Absorbed and often with their

52

mouths full, frequently with imperfect articulation, but with deepening satisfaction as the steaks vanished and the method they'd use took form in their minds. It wouldn't be wholly simple, of course. When the rotors were spinning about their centers of gravity, trimming off the shaft would change the center of gravity. But the change would be infinitely less than trimming off the rotors' rims. If they spun the rotors and used an abrasive on the high side of the shaft as it turned....

"Going to have precession!" warned Mike. "Have to have a polishing surface. Quarter turn behind the cutter. That'll hold it."

Joe only remembered afterward to be astonished that Mike would know gyro theory. At the moment he merely swallowed quickly to get the words out.

"Right! And if we cut too far down we can plate the bearing up to thickness and cut it down again——"

"Plate it up with iridium," said the Chief. He waved a steak knife. "Man! This is gonna be fun! No tolerance you say, Joe?"

"No tolerance," agreed Joe. "Accurate within the limits of measurement."

The Chief beamed. The Platform was a challenge to all of humanity. The pilot gyro was essential to the functioning of the Platform. To provide that necessity against impossible obstacles was a challenge to the four who were undertaking it.

"Some fun!" repeated the Chief, blissfully.

They ate their steaks, talking. They consumed huge slabs of apple pie with preposterous mounds of ice cream on top, still talking urgently. They drank coffee, interrupting each other to draw diagrams. They used up all the paper napkins, and were still at it when someone came heavily toward the table. It was the stocky man who had fought with Haney on the Platform that day. Braun.

He tapped Haney on the shoulder. The four at the table looked up.

"We hadda fight today," said Braun in a queer voice. He was oddly pale. "We didn't finish. You wanna finish?"

Haney growled.

"That was a fool business," he said angrily. "That ain't any place to fight, up on the job! You know it!"

53

"Yeah," said Braun in the same odd voice. "You wanna finish it now?"

Haney said formidably: "I'm not dodgin' any fight. I didn't dodge it then. I'm not dodgin' it now. You picked it. It was crazy! But if you got over the craziness— —"

Braun smiled a remarkably peculiar smile. "I'm still crazy. We finish, huh?"

Haney pushed back his chair and stood up grimly. "Okay, we finish it! You coulda killed me. I coulda killed you too, with that fall ready for either of us."

"Sure! Too bad nobody got killed," said Braun.

"You fellas wait," said Haney angrily to Joe and the rest. "There's a storeroom out back. Sid'll let us use it."

But the Chief pushed back his chair.

"Uh-uh," he said, shaking his head. "We're watchin' this."

Haney spoke with elaborate courtesy: "You mind, Braun? Want to get some friends of yours, too?"

"I got no friends," said Braun. "Let's go."

The Chief went authoritatively to the owner of Sid's Steak Joint. He paid the bill, talking. The owner of the place negligently jerked his thumb toward the rear. This was not an unparalleled request—for the use of a storeroom so that two men could batter each other undisturbed. Bootstrap was a law-abiding town, because to get fired from work on the Platform was to lose a place in the most important job in history. So it was inevitable that the settlement of quarrels in private should become commonplace.

The Chief leading, they filed through the kitchen and out of doors. The storeroom lay beyond. The Chief went in and switched on the light. He looked about and was satisfied. It was almost empty, save for stacked cartons in one corner. Braun was already taking off his coat.

"You want rounds and stuff?" demanded the Chief.

"I want fight," said Braun thickly.

"Okay, then," snapped the Chief. "No kickin' or gougin'. A man's down, he has a chance to get up. That's all the rules. Right?"

Haney, stripping off his coat in turn, grunted an assent. He handed his coat to Joe. He faced his antagonist.

It was a curious atmosphere for a fight. There were merely the plank walls of the storeroom with a single dangling light in the middle and an unswept floor beneath. The Chief stood in the doorway, scowling. This didn't feel right. There was not enough hatred in evidence to justify it. There was doggedness and resolution enough, but Braun was deathly white and if his face was contorted—and it was—it was not with the lust to batter and injure and maim. It was something else.

The two men faced each other. And then the stocky, swarthy Braun swung at Haney. The blow had sting in it but nothing more. It almost looked as if Braun were trying to work himself up to the fight he'd insisted on finishing. Haney countered with a roundhouse blow that glanced off Braun's cheek. And then they bore in at each other, slugging without science or skill.

Joe watched. Braun launched a blow that hurt, but Haney sent him reeling back. He came in doggedly again, and swung and swung, but he had no idea of boxing. His only idea was to slug. He did slug. Haney had been peevish rather than angry. Now he began to glower. He began to take the fight to Braun.

He knocked Braun down. Braun staggered up and rushed. A wildly flailing fist landed on Haney's ear. He doubled Braun up with a wallop to the midsection. Braun came back, fists swinging.

Haney closed one eye for him. He came back. Haney shook him from head to foot with a chest blow. He came back. Haney split his lip and loosened a tooth. He came back.

The Chief said sourly: "This ain't a fight. Quit it, Haney! He don't know how!"

Haney tried to draw away, but Braun swarmed on him, striking fiercely until Haney had to floor him again. He dragged himself up and rushed at Haney—and was knocked down again. Haney stood over him, panting furiously.

"Quit it, y'fool! What's the matter with you?"

Braun started to get up again. The Chief interfered and held him, while Haney glared.

"He ain't going to fight any more, Braun," pronounced the Chief firmly. "You ain't got a chance. This fight's over. You had enough."

Braun was bloody and horribly battered, but he panted: "He's got enough?"

"Are you out o' your head?" demanded the Chief. "He ain't got a mark on him!"

"I ain't—got enough," panted Braun, "till he's got—enough!"

His breath was coming in soblike gasps, the result of body blows. It hadn't been a fight but a beating, administered by Haney. But Braun struggled to get up.

Mike the midget said brittlely: "You got enough, Haney. You're satisfied. Tell him so."

"Sure I'm satisfied," snorted Haney. "I don't want to hit him any more. I got enough of that!"

Braun panted: "Okay! Okay!"

The Chief let him get to his feet. He went groggily to his coat. He tried to put himself into it. Mike caught Joe's eye and nodded meaningfully. Joe helped Braun into the coat. There was silence, save for Braun's heavy, labored breathing.

He moved unsteadily toward the door. Then he stopped.

"Haney," he said effortfully, "I don't say I'm sorry for fighting you today. I fight first. But now I say I am sorry. You are good guy, Haney. I was crazy. I—got reason."

He stumbled out of the door and was gone. The four who were left behind stared at each other.

"What's the matter with him?" demanded Haney blankly.

"He's nuts," said the Chief. "If he was gonna apologize——"

Mike shook his head.

"He wouldn't apologize," he said brittlely, "because he thought you might think he was scared. But when he'd proved he wasn't scared of a beating—then he could say he was sorry." He paused. "I've seen guys I liked a lot less than him."

Haney put on his coat, frowning.

"I don't get it," he rumbled. "Next time I see him——"

"You won't," snapped Mike. "None of us will. I'll bet on it."

But he was wrong. The others went out of the storeroom and back into Sid's Steak Joint, and the Chief politely thanked the proprietor for the loan of his storeroom for a private fight. Then they went out into the neon-lighted business street of Bootstrap.

"What do we do now?" asked Joe.

"Where you sleeping?" asked the Chief hospitably. "I can get you a room at my place."

"I'm staying out at the Shed," Joe told him awkwardly. "My family's known Major Holt a long time. I'm staying at his house behind the Shed."

Haney raised his eyebrows but said nothing.

"Better get out there then," said the Chief. "It's midnight, and they might want to lock up. There's your bus."

A lighted bus was waiting by the curb. Its doors were open, but it was empty of passengers. Single busses ran out to the Shed now and then, but they ran in fleets at shift-change time. Joe went over and climbed aboard the bus.

"We'll turn up early," said the Chief. "This won't be a shift job. We'll look things over and lay out what we want and then get to work, eh?"

"Right," said Joe. "And thanks."

"We'll be there with our hair in braids," said Mike, in his cracked voice. "Now a glass of beer and so to bed. 'Night."

Haney waved his hand. The three of them marched off, the two huge figures of Haney and the Chief, with Mike trotting truculently between them, hardly taller than their knees. They were curiously colorful with all the many-tinted neon signs upon them. They turned into a diner.

Joe sat in the bus, alone. The driver was off somewhere. The sounds of Bootstrap were distinctive by night. Footsteps, and the jangling of bicycle bells, and voices, and a radio blaring somewhere and a record-shop loud-speaker somewhere else, and a sort of underriding noise of festivity.

There was a sharp rap on the glass by Joe's window. He started and looked out. Braun—battered, and bleeding from the corner of his mouth—motioned urgently for him to come to the door of the bus. Joe went.

Braun stared up at him in a new fashion. Now he was neither dogged nor fierce nor desperate to look at. Despite the beating he'd taken, he seemed completely and somehow frighteningly tranquil.

57

He looked like somebody who has come to the end of torment and is past any feeling but that of relief from suffering.

"You—" said Braun. "That girl you were with today. Her pop is Major Holt, eh?"

Joe frowned, and reservedly said that he was.

"You tell her pop," said Braun detachedly, "this is hot tip. Hot tip. Look two kilometers north of Shed tomorrow. He find something bad. Hot! You tell him. Two kilometers."

"Y-yes," said Joe, his frown increasing. "But look here——"

"Be sure say hot," repeated Braun.

Rather incredibly, he smiled. Then he turned and walked quickly away.

Joe went back to his seat in the empty bus, and sat there and waited for it to start, and tried to figure out what the message meant. Since it was for Major Holt, it had something to do with security. And security meant defense against sabotage. And "hot" might mean merely significant, or—in these days—it might mean something else. In fact, it might mean something to make your hair stand on end when thought of in connection with the Space Platform.

Joe waited for the bus to take off. He became convinced that Braun's use of the word "hot" did not mean merely "significant." The other meaning was what he had in mind.

Joe's teeth tried to chatter.

He didn't let them.

CHAPTER 6

Major Holt wasn't to be found when Joe got out to the Shed. And he wasn't in the house in the officers'-quarters area behind it. There was only the housekeeper, who yawned pointedly as she let Joe in. Sally was presumably long since asleep. And Joe didn't know any way to get hold of the Major. He assured himself that Braun was a good guy—if he weren't he wouldn't have insisted on taking a licking before he apologized—and he hadn't said there was any hurry. Tomorrow, he'd said. So Joe uneasily let himself be led to a room with a cot, and he was asleep in what seemed seconds. But just the same he was badly worried.

In fact, next morning Joe woke at a practically unearthly hour with Braun's message pounding on his brain. He was downstairs waiting when the housekeeper appeared. She looked startled.

"Major Holt?" he asked.

But the Major was gone. He must have done with no more than three or four hours' sleep. There was an empty coffee cup whose contents he'd gulped down before going back to the security office.

Joe trudged to the barbed-wire enclosure around the officers'-quarters area and explained to the sentry where he wanted to go. A sleepy driver whisked him around the half-mile circle to the security building and he found his way to Major Holt's office.

The plain and gloomy secretary was already on the job, too. She led him in to face Major Holt. He blinked at the sight of Joe.

"Hm.... I have some news," he observed. "We back-tracked the parcel that exploded when it was dumped from the plane."

Joe had almost forgotten it. Too many other things had happened since.

"We've got two very likely prisoners out of that affair," said the Major. "They may talk. Also, an emergency inspection of other transport planes has turned up three other grenades tucked away in front-wheel wells. Ah—CO_2 bottles have turned out to have something explosive in them. A very nice bit of work, that! The sandy-haired man who fueled your plane—ah—disappeared. That is bad!"

Joe said politely: "That's fine, sir."

"All in all, you've been the occasion of our forestalling a good deal of sabotage," said the Major. "Bad for you, of course.... Did you find the men you were looking for?"

"I've found them, but—."

"I'll have them transferred to work under your direction," said the Major briskly. "Their names?"

Joe gave the names. The Major wrote them down.

"Very good. I'm busy now——"

"I've a tip for you," said Joe. "I think it should be checked right away. I don't feel too good about it."

The Major waited impatiently. And Joe explained, very carefully, about the fight on the Platform the day before, Braun's insistence on finishing the fight in Bootstrap, and then the tip he'd given Joe after everything was over. He repeated the message exactly, word for word.

The Major, to do him justice, did not interrupt. He listened with an expression that varied between grimness and weariness. When Joe ended he picked up a telephone. He talked briefly. Joe felt a reluctant sort of approval. Major Holt was not a man one could ever feel very close to, and the work he was in charge of was not likely to make him popular, but he did think straight—and fast. He didn't think "hot" meant "significant," either. When he'd hung up the phone he said curtly: "When will your work crew get here?"

"Early—but not yet," said Joe. "Not for some time yet."

"Go with the pilot," said the Major. "You'd recognize what Braun meant as soon as anybody. See what you see."

Joe stood up.

"You—think the tip is straight?"

"This isn't the first time," said Major Holt detachedly, "that a man has been blackmailed into trying sabotage. If he's got a family somewhere abroad, and they're threatened with death or torture unless he does such-and-such here, he's in a bad fix. It's happened. Of course he can't tell me! He's watched. But he sometimes finds an out."

Joe was puzzled. His face showed it.

"He can try to do the sabotage," said the Major precisely, "or

60

he can arrange to be caught trying to do it. If he's caught—he tried; and the blackmail threat is no threat at all so long as he keeps his mouth shut. Which he does. And—ah—you would be surprised how often a man who wasn't born in the United States would rather go to prison for sabotage than commit it—here."

Joe blinked.

"If your friend Braun is caught," said the Major, "he will be punished. Severely. Officially. But privately, someone will—ah—mention this tip and say 'thanks.' And he'll be told that he will be released from prison just as soon as he thinks it's safe. And he will be. That's all."

He turned to his papers. Joe went out. On the way to meet the pilot who'd check on his tip, he thought things over. He began to feel a sort of formless but very definite pride. He wasn't quite sure what he was proud of, but it had something to do with being part of a country toward which men of wholly different upbringing could feel deep loyalty. If a man who was threatened unless he turned traitor, a man who might not even be a citizen, arranged to be caught and punished for an apparent crime against a country rather than commit it—that wasn't bad. There can be a lot of things wrong with a nation, but if somebody from another one entirely can come to feel that kind of loyalty toward it—well—it's not too bad a country to belong to.

Joe had a security guard with him this time, instead of Sally, as he went across the vast, arc-lit interior of the Shed and past the shimmering growing monster that was the Platform. He went all the way to the great swinging doors that let in materials trucks. And there were guards there, and they checked each driver very carefully before they admitted his truck. But somehow it wasn't irritating. It wasn't scornful suspicion. There'd be snide and snappy characters in the Security force, of course, swaggering and throwing their weight about. But even they were guarding something that men—some men—were willing to throw away their lives for.

Joe and his guard reached one of the huge entrances as a ten-wheeler truck came in with a load of shining metal plates. Joe's escort went through the opening with him and they waited outside. The sun had barely risen. It looked huge but very far away, and Joe

61

suddenly realized why just this spot had been chosen for the building of the Platform.

The ground was flat. All the way to the eastern horizon there wasn't even a minor hillock rising above the plain. It was bare, arid, sun-scorched desert. It was featureless save for sage and mesquite and tall thin stalks of yucca. But it was flat. It could be a runway. It was a perfect place for the Platform to start from. The Platform shouldn't touch ground at all, after it was out of the Shed, but at least it wouldn't run into any obstacles on its way toward the horizon.

A light plane came careening around the great curved outer surface of the Shed. It landed and taxied up to the door. It swung smartly around and its side door opened. A bandaged hand waved at Joe. He climbed in. The pilot of this light, flimsy plane was the co-pilot of the transport of yesterday. He was the man Joe had helped to dump cargo.

Joe climbed in and settled himself. The small motor pop-popped valiantly, the plane rushed forward over hard-packed desert earth, and went swaying up into the air.

The co-pilot—pilot now—shouted cheerfully above the din: "Hiya. You couldn't sleep either? Burns hurt?"

Joe shook his head.

"Bothered," he shouted in reply. Then he added, "Do I do something to help, or am I along just for the ride?"

"First we take a look," the pilot called over the motor racket. "Two kilometers due north of the Shed, eh?"

"That's right."

"We'll see what's there," the pilot told him.

The small plane went up and up. At five hundred feet—nearly level with the roof of the Shed—it swung away and began to make seemingly erratic dartings out over the spotty desert land, and then back. Actually, it was a search pattern. Joe looked down from his side of the small cockpit. This was a very small plane indeed, and in consequence its motor made much more noise inside its cabin than much more powerful engines in bigger ships.

"Those burns I got," shouted the pilot, staring down, "kept me

62

awake. So I got up and was just walking around when the call came for somebody to drive one of these things. I took over."

Back and forth, and back and forth. From five hundred feet in the early morning the desert had a curious appearance. The plane was low enough for each smallest natural feature to be visible, and it was early enough for every shrub or hummock to cast a long, slender shadow. The ground looked streaked, but all the streaks ran the same way, and all were shadows.

Joe shouted: "What's that?"

The plane banked at a steep angle and ran back. It banked again. The pilot stared carefully. He reached forward and pushed a button. There was a tiny impact underfoot. Another steep banking turn, and Joe saw a puff of smoke in the air.

The pilot shouted: "It's a man. He looks dead."

He swung directly over the small prone object and there was a second puff of smoke.

"They've got range finders on us from the Shed," he called across the two-foot space separating him from Joe. "This marks the spot. Now we'll see if there's anything to the hot part of that tip."

He reached over behind his seat and brought out a stubby pole like a fishpole with a very large reel. There was also a headset, and something very much like a large aluminum fish on the end of the line.

"You know Geiger counters?" called the pilot. "Stick on these headphones and listen!"

Joe slipped on the headset. The pilot threw a switch and Joe heard clickings. They had no pattern and no fixed frequency. They were clickings at strictly random intervals, but there was an average frequency, at that.

"Let the counter out the window," called the pilot, "and listen. Tell me if the noise goes up."

Joe obeyed. The aluminum fish dangled. The line slanted astern from the wind. It made a curve between the pole and the aluminum plummet, which was hollow in the direction of the plane's motion. The pilot squinted down and began to swing in a wide circle around the spot where an apparently dead man had been sighted, and above which puffs of smoke now floated.

Three-quarters of the way around, the random clickings suddenly became a roar.

Joe said: "Hey!"

The pilot swung the plane about and flew back. He pointed to the button he'd pushed.

"Poke that when you hear it again."

The clickings.... They roared. Joe pushed the button. He felt the tiny impact.

"Once more," said the pilot.

He swung in nearer where the dead man lay. Joe had a sickening idea of who the dead man might be. A sudden rush of noise in the headphones and he pushed the button again.

"Reel in now!" shouted the pilot. "Our job's done."

Joe reeled in as the plane winged steadily back toward the Shed. There were puffs of smoke floating in the air behind. They had been ranged on at the instant they appeared. Somebody back at the Shed knew that something that needed to be investigated was at a certain spot, and the two later puffs of smoke had said that radioactivity was notable in the air along the line the two puffs made. Not much more information would be needed. The meaning of Braun's warning that his tip was "hot" was definite. It was "hot" in the sense that it dealt with radioactivity!

The plane dipped down and landed by the great doors again. It taxied up and the pilot killed the motor.

"We've been using Geigers for months," he said pleasedly, "and never got a sign before. This is one time we were set for something."

"What?" asked Joe. But he knew.

"Atomic dust is one good guess," the pilot told him. "It was talked of as a possible weapon away back in the Smyth Report. Nobody's ever tried it. We thought it might be tried against the Platform. If somebody managed to spread some really hot radioactive dust around the Shed, all three shifts might get fatally burned before it was noticed. They'd think so, anyhow! But the guy who was supposed to dump it opened up the can for a look. And it killed him."

64

He climbed out of the plane and went to the doorway. He took a telephone from a guard and talked crisply into it. He hung up.

"Somebody coming for you," he said amiably. "Wait here. Be seeing you."

He went out, the motor kicked over and caught, and the tiny plane raced away. Seconds later it was aloft and winging southward.

Joe waited. Presently a door opened and something came clanking out. It was a tractor with surprisingly heavy armor. There were men in it, also wearing armor of a peculiar sort, which they were still adjusting. The tractor towed a half-track platform on which there were a crane and a very considerable lead-coated bin with a top. It went briskly off into the distance toward the north.

Joe was amazed, but comprehending. The vehicle and the men were armored against radioactivity. They would approach the dead man from upwind, and they would scoop up his body and put it in the lead-lined bin, and with it all deadly radioactive material near him. This was the equipment that must have been used to handle the dud atom bomb some months back. It had been ready for that. It was ready for this emergency. Somebody had tried to think of every imaginable situation that could arise in connection with the Platform.

But in a moment a guard came for Joe and took him to where the Chief and Haney and Mike waited by the still incompletely-pulled-away crates. They had some new ideas about the job on hand that were better than the original ones in some details. All four of them set to work to make a careful survey of damage—of parts that would have to be replaced and of those that needed to be repaired. The discoveries they made would have appalled Joe earlier. Now he merely made notes of parts necessary to be replaced by new ones that could be had within the repair time for rebalancing the rotors.

"This is sure a mess," said Haney mournfully, as they worked. "It's two days just getting things cleaned up!"

The Chief eyed the rotors. There were two of them, great four-foot disks with extraordinary short and stubby shafts that were brought to beautifully polished conical ends to fit in the bearings.

65

The bearings were hollowed to fit the shaft ends, but they were intricately scored to form oil channels. In operation, a very special silicone oil would be pumped into the bearings under high pressure. Distributed by the channels, the oil would form a film that by its pressure would hold the cone end of the bearing away from actual contact with the metal. The rotors, in fact, would be floated in oil just as the high-speed centrifuge the Chief had mentioned had floated on compressed air. But they had to be perfectly balanced, because any imbalance would make the shaft pierce the oil film and touch the metal of the bearing—and when a shaft is turning at 40,000 r.p.m. it is not good for it to touch anything. Shaft and bearing would burn white-hot in fractions of a second and there would be several devils to pay.

"We've got to spin it in a lathe," said the Chief profoundly, "to hold the chucks. The chucks have got to be these same bearings, because nothing else will stand the speed. And we got to cut out the bed plate of any lathe we find. Hm. We got to do our spinning with the shaft lined up with the earth's axis, too."

Mike nodded wisely, and Joe knew he'd pointed that out. It was true enough. A high-speed gyro could only be run for minutes in one single direction if its mount were fixed. If a precisely mounted gyro had its shaft pointed at the sun, for example, while it ran, its axis would try to follow the sun. It would try not to turn with the earth, and it would wreck itself. They had to use the cone bearings, but in order to protect the fine channellings for oil they'd have to use cone-shaped shims at the beginning while running at low speed. The cone ends of the shaft would need new machining to line them up. The bearings had to be fixed, yet flexible. The——

They had used many paper napkins the night before, merely envisioning these details. New problems turned up as the apparatus itself was being uncovered and cleaned.

They worked for hours, clearing away soot and charred material. Joe's list of small parts to be replaced from the home plant was as long as his arm. The motors, of course, had to be scrapped and new ones substituted. Considering their speed—the field strength at operating rate was almost imperceptible—they had to be built new, which would mean round-the-clock work at Kenmore.

A messenger came for Joe. The security office wanted him. Major Holt's gloomy secretary did not even glance up as he entered. Major Holt himself looked tired.

"There was a man out there," he said curtly. "I think it is your friend Braun. I'll get you to look and identify."

Joe had suspected as much. He waited.

"He'd opened a container of cobalt powder. It was in a beryllium case. There was half a pound of it. It killed him."

"Radioactive cobalt," said Joe.

"Definitely," said the Major grimly. "Half a pound of it gives off the radiation of an eighth of a ton of pure radium. One can guess that he had been instructed to get up as high as he could in the Shed and dump the powder into the air. It would diffuse—scatter as it sifted down. It would have contaminated the whole Shed past all use for years—let alone killing everybody in it."

Joe swallowed.

"He was burned, then."

"He had the equivalent of two hundred and fifty pounds of radium within inches of his body," the Major said unbendingly, "and naturally it was not healthy. For that matter, the container itself was not adequate protection for him. Once he'd carried it in his pocket for a very few minutes, he was a dead man, even though he was not conscious of the fact."

Joe knew what was wanted of him.

"You want me to look at him," he said.

The Major nodded.

"Yes. Afterward, get a radiation check on yourself. It is hardly likely that he was—ah—carrying the stuff with him last night, in Bootstrap. But if he was—ah—you may need some precautionary treatment—you and the men who were with you."

Joe realized what that meant. Braun had been given a relatively small container of the deadliest available radioactive material on Earth. Milligrams of it, shipped from Oak Ridge for scientific use, were encased in thick lead chests. He'd carried two hundred and fifty grams in a container he could put in his pocket. He was not only dead as he walked, under such circumstances. He was also death to those who walked near him.

67

"Somebody else may have been burned in any case," said the Major detachedly. "I am going to issue a radioactivity alarm and check every man in Bootstrap for burns. It is—ah—very likely that the man who delivered it to this man is burned, too. But you will not mention this, of course."

He waved his hand in dismissal. Joe turned to go. The Major added grimly: "By the way, there is no doubt about the booby-trapping of planes. We've found eight, so far, ready to be crashed when a string was pulled while they were serviced. But the men who did the booby-trapping have vanished. They disappeared suddenly during last night. They were warned! Have you talked to anybody?"

"No sir," said Joe.

"I would like to know," said the Major coldly, "how they knew we'd found out their trick!"

Joe went out. He felt very cold at the pit of his stomach. He was to identify Braun. Then he was to get a radiation check on himself. In that order of events. He was to identify Braun first, because if Braun had carried a half-pound of radioactive cobalt on him in Sid's Steak Joint the night before, Joe was going to die. And so were Haney and the Chief and Mike, and anybody else who'd passed near him. So Joe was to do the identification before he was disturbed by the information that he was dead.

He made the identification. Braun was very decently laid out in a lead-lined box, with a lead-glass window over his face. There was no sign of any injury on him except from his fight with Haney. The radiation burns were deep, but they'd left no marks of their own. He'd died before outer symptoms could occur.

Joe signed the identification certificate. He went to be checked for his own chances of life. It was a peculiar sensation. The most peculiar was that he wasn't afraid. He was neither confident that he was not burned inside, nor sure that he was. He simply was not afraid. Nobody really ever believes that he is going to die—in the sense of ceasing to exist. The most arrant coward, stood before a wall to be shot, or strapped in an electric chair, finds that astoundingly he does not believe that what happens to his body is going to kill him, the individual. That is why a great many people

68

die with reasonable dignity. They know it is not worth making too much of a fuss over.

But when the Geiger counters had gone over him from head to foot, and his body temperature was normal, and his reflexes sound—when he was assured that he had not been exposed to dangerous radiation—Joe felt distinctly weak in the knees. And that was natural, too.

He went trudging back to the wrecked gyros. His friends were gone, leaving a scrawled memo for him. They had gone to pick out the machine tools for the work at hand.

He continued to check over the wreckage, thinking with a detached compassion of that poor devil Braun who was the victim of men who hated the idea of the Space Platform and what it would mean to humanity. Men of that kind thought of themselves as superior to humanity, and of human beings as creatures to be enslaved. So they arranged for planes to crash and burn and for men to be murdered, and they practiced blackmail—or rewarded those who practiced it for them. They wanted to prevent the Platform from existing because it would keep them from trying to pull the world down in ruins so they could rule over the wreckage.

Joe—who had so recently thought it likely that he would die—considered these actions with an icy dislike that was much deeper than anger. It was backed by everything he believed in, everything he had ever wanted, and everything he hoped for. And anger could cool off, but the way he felt about people who would destroy others for their own purposes could not cool off. It was part of him. He thought about it as he worked, with all the noises of the Shed singing in his ears.

A voice said: "Joe."

He started and turned. Sally stood behind him, looking at him very gravely. She tried to smile.

"Dad told me," she said, "about the check-up that says you're all right. May I congratulate you on your being with us for a while?—on the cobalt's not getting near you?—or the rest of us?"

Joe did not know exactly what to say.

"I'm going inside the Platform," she told him. "Would you like to come along?"

69

He wiped his hands on a piece of waste.

"Naturally! My gang is off picking out tools. I can't do much until they come back."

He fell into step beside her. They walked toward the Platform. And it was still magic, no matter how often Joe looked at it. It was huge beyond belief, though it was surely not heavy in proportion to its size. Its bright plating shone through the gossamer scaffolding all about it. There was always a faint bluish mist in the air, and there were the marsh-fire lights of welding torches playing here and there. The sounds of the Shed were a steady small tumult in Joe's ears. He was getting accustomed to them, though.

"How is it you can go around so freely?" he asked abruptly. "I have to be checked and rechecked."

"You'll get a full clearance," she told him. "It has to go through channels. Me—I have influence. I always come in through security, and I have the door guards trained. And I do have business in the Platform."

He turned his head to look at her.

"Interior decoration," she explained. "And don't laugh! It isn't prettifying. It's psychology. The Platform was designed by engineers and physicists and people with slide rules. They made a beautiful environment for machinery. But there will be men living in it, and they aren't machines."

"I don't see——"

"They designed the hydroponic garden," said Sally with a certain scorn. "They calculated very neatly that eleven square feet of leaf surface of a pumpkin plant will purify all the air a resting man uses, and so much more will purify the air a man uses when he's working hard. So they designed the gardens for the most efficient production of the greatest possible leaf surface—of pumpkin plants! They figured food would be brought up by the tender rockets! But can you imagine the men in the Platform, floating among the stars, living on dehydrated food and stuffing themselves hungrily with pumpkins because that is the only fresh food they have?"

Joe saw the irony.

"They're thinking of mechanical efficiency," said Sally

indignantly. "I don't know anything about machinery, but I've wasted an awful lot of time at school and otherwise if I don't know something about human beings! I argued, and the garden now isn't as mechanically efficient, but it'll be a nice place for a man to go into. He won't smell pumpkin plants all the time, either. I've even gotten them to include some flowers!"

They were very near the Platform. And it was very near to completion. Joe looked at it hungrily, and he felt a great sense of urgency. He tried to strip away the scaffolding in his mind and see it floating proudly free in emptiness, with white-hot sunshine glinting from it, and only a background of unwinking stars.

Sally's voice went on: "And I've really put up an argument about the living quarters. They had every interior wall painted aluminum! I argued that in space or out of it, where people have to live, it's housekeeping. This is going to be their home. And they ought to feel human in it!"

They passed into one of the openings in the maze of uprights. All about them there were trucks, and puffing engines, and hoists. Joe dragged Sally aside as a monstrous truck-and-trailer came from where it had delivered some gigantic item of interior use. It rumbled past them, and she led the way to a flight of temporary wooden stairs with two security guards at the bottom. Sally talked severely to them, and they grinned and waved for Joe to go ahead. He went up the steps—which would be pulled down before the Platform's launching—and went actually inside the Space Platform for the first time.

It was a moment of extreme vividness for him. Within the past hour he'd come to think detachedly of the possibility of death for himself, and then had learned that he would live for a while yet. He knew that Sally had been scared on his account, and that her matter-of-fact manner was partly assumed. She was at least as much wrought up as he was.

And this was the first time he was going into what would be the first space ship ever to leave the Earth on a non-return journey.

CHAPTER 7

Nobody could have gone through the changes of emotion Joe had experienced that morning and remained quite matter-of-fact. Seeing a dead man who had more or less deliberately killed himself so that he wouldn't have to kill Joe—for one—had its effect. Knowing that it was certainly possible the man hadn't killed himself in time had another. Being checked over for radiation burns which would mean that he'd die quite comfortably within three or four days, and then learning that no burns existed, was something of an ordeal. And Sally—of course her feelings shouldn't have been as vivid as his own, but the fact that she'd been scared for him held some significance. When, on top of all the rest, he went into the Space Platform for the first time, Joe was definitely keyed up.

But he talked technology. He examined the inner skin and its lining before going beyond the temporary entrance. The plating of the Platform was actually double. The outer layer was a meteor-bumper against which particles of cosmic dust would strike and explode without damage to the inner skin. They could even penetrate it without causing a leak of air. Inside the inner skin there was a layer of glass wool for heat insulation. Inside the glass wool was a layer of material serving exactly the function of the coating of a bulletproof gasoline tank. No meteor under a quarter-inch size could hope to make a puncture, even at the forty-five-mile-per-second speed that is the theoretical maximum for meteors. And if one did, the selfsealing stuff would stop the leak immediately. Joe could explain the protection of the metal skins. He did.

"When a missile travels fast enough," he said absorbedly, "it stops acquiring extra puncturing ability. Over a mile a second, impact can't be transmitted from front to rear. The back end of the thing that hits has arrived at the hit place before the shock of arrival can travel back to it. It's like a train in a collision which doesn't stop all at once. A meteor hitting the Platform will telescope on itself like the cars of a railroad train that hits another at full speed."

Sally listened enigmatically.

"So," said Joe, "the punching effect isn't there. A meteor hitting

72

the Platform won't punch. It'll explode. Part of it will turn to vapor—metallic vapor if it's metal, and rocky vapor if it's stone. It'll blow a crater in the metal plate. It'll blow away as much weight of the skin as it weighs itself. Mass for mass. So that weight for weight, pea soup would be just as effective armor against meteors as hardened steel."

Sally said: "Dear me! You must read the newspapers!"

"The odds figure out, the odds are even that the Platform won't get an actual meteor puncture in the first twenty thousand years it's floating round the Earth."

"Twenty thousand two seventy, Joe," said Sally. She was trying to tease him, but her face showed a little of the strain. "I read the magazine articles too. In fact I sometimes show the tame article writers around, when they're cleared to see the Platform."

Joe winced a little. Then he grinned wryly.

"That cuts me down to size, eh?"

She smiled at him. But they both felt queer. They went on into the interior of the huge space ship.

"Lots of space," said Joe. "This could've been smaller."

"It'll be nine-tenths empty when it goes up," said Sally. "But you know about that, don't you?"

Joe did know. The reasons for the streamlining of rockets to be fired from the ground didn't apply to the Platform. Not with the same urgency, anyhow. Rockets had to burn their fuel fast to get up out of the dense air near the ground. They had to be streamlined to pierce the thick, resisting part of the atmosphere. The Platform didn't. It wouldn't climb by itself. It would be carried necessarily at slow speed up to the point where jet motors were most efficient, and then it would be carried higher until they ceased to be efficient. Only when it was up where air resistance was a very small fraction of ground-level drag would its own rockets fire. It wouldn't gain much by being shaped to cut thin air, and it would lose a lot. For one thing, the launching process planned for the Platform allowed it to be built complete so far as its hull was concerned. Once it got out into its orbit there would be no more worries. There wouldn't be any gamble on the practicability of assembling a great structure in a weightless "world."

73

The two of them—and the way they both felt, it seemed natural for Joe to be helping Sally very carefully through the corridors of the Platform—the two of them came to the engine room. This wasn't the place where the drive of the Platform was centered. It was where the service motors and the air-circulation system and the fluid pumps were powered. Off the engine room the main gyros were already installed. They waited only for the pilot gyros to control them as a steering engine controls an Earth ship's rudder. Joe looked very thoughtfully at the gyro assembly. That was familiar, from the working drawings. But he let Sally guide him on without trying to stop and look closely.

She showed him the living quarters. They centered in a great open space sixty feet long and twenty wide and high. There were bookshelves, and two balconies, and chairs. Private cabins opened from it on different levels, but there were no steps to them. Yet there were comfortable chairs with straps so that when a man was weightless he could fasten himself in them. There were ash trays, ingeniously designed to look like exactly that and nothing else. But ashes would not fall into them, but would be drawn into them by suction. There was unpatterned carpet on the floor and on the ceiling.

"It's going to feel queer," said Sally, oddly quiet, "when all this is out in space, but it will look fairly normal. I think that's important. This room will look like a big private library more than anything else. One won't be reminded every second, by everything he sees, that he's living in a strictly synthetic environment. He won't feel cramped. If all the rooms were small, a man would feel as if he were in prison. At least this way he can pretend that things are normal."

Her mind was not wholly on her words. She'd been frightened for Joe. And he was acutely aware of it, because he felt a peculiar after-effect himself.

"Normal," he said drily, "except that he doesn't weigh anything."

"I've worried about that," said Sally. "Sleeping's going to be a big problem."

"It'll take getting used to," Joe agreed.

There was a momentary pause. They were simply looking about the great room. Sally stirred uneasily.

"Tell me what you think," she said. "You've been in an elevator that started to drop like a plummet. When the Platform is orbiting it'll be like that all the time, only worse. No weight. Joe, if you were in an elevator that seemed to be dropping and dropping and dropping for hours on end—do you think you could go to sleep?"

Joe hadn't thought about it. And he was acutely conscious of Sally, just then, but the idea startled him.

"It might be hard to adjust to," he admitted.

"It'll be hard to adjust to, awake," said Sally. "But getting adjusted to it asleep should be worse. You've waked up from a dream that you're falling?"

"Sure," said Joe. Then he whistled. "Oh-oh! I see! You'd drop off to sleep, and you'd be falling. So you'd wake up. Everybody in the Platform will be falling around the Earth in the Platform's orbit! Every time they doze off they'll be falling and they'll wake up!"

He managed to think about it. It was true enough. A man awake could remind himself that he only thought and felt that he was falling, and that there was no danger. But what would happen when he tried to sleep? Falling is the first fear a human being ever knows. Everybody in the world has at one time waked up gasping from a dream of precipices down which he plunged. It is an inborn terror. And no matter how thoroughly a man might know in his conscious mind that weightlessness was normal in emptiness, his conscious mind would go off duty when he went to sleep. A completely primitive subconscious would take over then, and it would not be satisfied. It might wake him frantically at any sign of dozing until he cracked up from sheer insomnia ... or else let him sleep only when exhaustion produced unconsciousness rather than restful slumber.

"That's a tough one!" he said disturbedly, and noticed that she still showed signs of her recent distress. "There's not much to be done about it, either!"

"I suggested something," said Sally, "and they built it in. I hope it works!" she explained uncomfortably. "It's a sort of blanket with a top that straps down, and an inflatable underside. When a man wants to sleep, he'll inflate this thing, and it will hold him in his bunk. It won't touch his head, of course, and he can move, but it will press against him gently."

Joe thought over what Sally had just explained. He noticed that they were quite close together, but he put his mind on her words.

"It'll be like a man swimming?" he asked. "One can go to sleep floating. There's no sensation of weight, but there's the feeling of pressure all about. A man might be able to sleep if he felt he were floating. Yes, that's a good idea, Sally! It'll work! A man will think he's floating, rather than falling!"

Sally flushed a little.

"I thought of it another way," she said awkwardly. "When we go to sleep, we go way back. We're like babies, with all a baby's fears and needs. It might feel like floating. But—I tried one of those bunks. It feels like—it feels sort of dreamy, as if someone were—holding one quite safe. It feels as if one were a baby and—beautifully secure. But of course I haven't tried it weightless. I just—hope it works."

As if embarrassed, she turned abruptly and showed him the kitchen. Every pan was covered. The top of the stove was alnico-magnet strips, arranged rather like the top of a magnetic chuck. Pans would cling to it. And the covers had a curious flexible lining which Joe could not understand.

"It's a flexible plastic that's heatproof," said Sally. "It inflates and holds the food down to the hot bottom of the pan. They expected the crew to eat ready-prepared food. I said that it would be bad enough to have to drink out of plastic bottles instead of glasses. They hung one of these stoves upside down, for me, and I cooked bacon and eggs and pancakes with the cover of the pan pointing to the floor. They said the psychological effect would be worth while."

Joe was stirred. He followed her out of the kitchen and said warmly—the more warmly because these contributions to the Space Platform came on top of a personal anxiety on his own account: "You must be the first girl in the world who thought about housekeeping in space!"

76

"Girls will be going into space, won't they?" she asked, not looking at him. "If there are colonies on the other planets, they'll have to. And some day—to the stars...."

She stood quite still, and Joe wanted to do something about her and the world and the way he felt. The interior of the Platform was very silent. Somewhere far away where the glass-wool insulation was incomplete, the sound of workmen was audible, but the inner corridors of the Platform were not resonant. They were lined with a material to destroy reminders that this was merely a metal shell, an artificial world that would swim in emptiness. Here and now, Joe and Sally seemed very private and alone, and he felt a sense of urgency.

He looked at her yearningly. Her color was a little higher than usual. She was not just a nice kid, she was swell! And she was good to look at. Joe had noticed that before, but now with the memory of her fright because he'd been in danger, her worry because he might have been killed, he thought of her very absurd but honest offer to cry for him.

Joe found himself twisting at the ring on his finger. He got it off, and there was some soot and grease on it from the work he'd been doing. He knew that she saw what he was about, but she looked away.

"Look, Sally," he said awkwardly, "we've known each other a long time. I've—uh—liked you a lot. And I've got some things to do first, but——" He stopped. He swallowed. She turned and smiled at him. "Look," he said desperately, "what's a good way to ask if you'd like to wear this?"

She nodded, her eyes shining a little.

"That was a good way, Joe. I'd like it a lot."

There was an interlude, then, during which she very ridiculously cried and explained that he must be more careful and not risk his life so much! And then there was a faint, faint sound outside the Platform. It was the yapping sound of a siren, crying out in short and choppy ululations as it warmed up. Finally its note steadied and it wailed and wailed and wailed.

"That's the alarm," exclaimed Sally. She was still misty-eyed. "Everybody out of the Shed. Come on, Joe."

They started back the way they'd come in. And Sally looked up at Joe and grinned suddenly.

"When I have grandchildren," she told him, "I'm going to brag that I was the very first girl in all the world ever to be kissed in a space ship!"

But before Joe could do anything about the comment, she was out on the stairs, in plain view and going down. So he followed her.

The Shed was emptying. The bare wood-block floor was dotted with figures moving steadily toward the security exit. There was no hurry, because security men were shouting that this was not an alarm but a precautionary measure, and there was no need for haste. Each security man had been informed by the miniature walkie-talkie he wore. By it every guard could be told anything he needed to know, either on the floor of the Shed, or on the catwalks aloft or even in the Platform itself.

Trucks lined up in orderly fashion to go out the swing-up doors. Men came down from the scaffolds after putting their tools in proper between-shifts positions—for counting and inspection—and other men were streaming quietly from the pushpot assembly line. Except for the gigantic object in the middle, and for the fact that every man was in work clothes, the scene was surprisingly like the central waiting room of a very large railroad station, with innumerable people moving briskly here and there.

"No hurry," said Joe, catching the word from a security man as he passed it on. "I'll go see what my gang found out."

The trio—Haney and Mike and the Chief—were just arriving by the piles of charred but now uncovered wreckage. Sally flushed ever so slightly when she saw the Chief eye Joe's ring on her finger.

"Rest of the day off, huh?" said the Chief. "Look! We found most of the stuff we need. They're gonna give us a shop to work in. We'll move this stuff there. We're gonna have to weld a false frame on the lathe we picked, an' then cut out the bed plate to let the gyros fit in between the chucks. Mount it so the spinning is in the right line."

That would be with the axis of the rotors parallel to the axis of the earth. Joe nodded.

"We'll be able to get set up in the mornin'," added Haney, "and

78

get started. You got the parts list off to the plant for your folks to get busy on?"

Sally said quickly: "He's sending that by facsimile now. Then-"

The Chief beamed in benign mockery. "What you goin' to do after that, Joe? If we got the rest of the day off— —?"

Sally said hurriedly: "We were—he was going off on a picnic with me. To Red Canyon Lake. Do you really need to talk business—all afternoon?"

The Chief laughed. He'd known Sally, at least by sight, back at the Kenmore plant.

"No, ma'am!" he told her. "Just askin'. I worked on that Red Canyon dam job, years back. That dam that made the lake. It ought to be right pretty around there now. Okay, Joe. See you as soon as work starts up. In the mornin', most likely."

Joe started away with Sally. Mike the midget called hoarsely: "Joe! Just a minute!"

Joe drew back. The midget's seamed face was very earnest. He said in his odd voice: "Here's something to think about. Somebody worked mighty hard to keep you from getting those gyros here. They might work hard to keep them from getting repaired. That's why we asked for a special shop to work in. It's occurred to me that a good way to stop these repairs would be to stop us. Not everybody would've figured out how to rebalance this thing. You get me?"

"Sure!" said Joe. "You three had better look out for yourselves."

Mike stared at him and grimaced.

"You don't get it," he said brittlely. "All right. I may be crazy, at that."

Joe rejoined Sally. The idea of a picnic was brand new to him, but he approved of it completely. They went to the small exit that led to the security building. They were admitted. There was remarkable calm and efficiency here, even though routine had been upset by the need to stop all work. As they went toward Major Holt's office, Joe heard somebody dictating in a matter-of-fact voice: "... this attempt at atomic sabotage was defeated outside the Shed, but it never had a chance of success. Geiger counters would have

79

instantly shown any attempt to smuggle radioactive material into the Shed...."

Joe glanced sidewise at Sally.

"That's for a publicity release?" he asked.

She nodded.

"It's true, too. Nothing goes in or out of the Shed without passing close to a Geiger counter. Even radium-dial watches show up, though they don't set the sirens to screaming."

Joe said: "I'll get my order for new parts off on the facsimile machine."

But he had to get Major Holt's secretary to show him where to feed in the list. It would go east to the nearest facsimile receiver, and then be rushed by special messenger to the plant. Miss Ross gloomily set the machine and initialed the delivery requisition which was part of the document. It flashed through the scanning process and came out again.

"You and Sally," remarked Sally's father's secretary with a morose sigh, "can go and relax this afternoon. But there's no relaxation for Major Holt. Or for me."

Joe said unhopefully: "I'm sure Sally'd be glad if you came with us."

Major Holt's plain, unglamorous assistant shook her head.

"I haven't had a day off since the work began here," she said frowning. "The Major depends on me. Nobody else could do what I do! You're going to Red Canyon Lake?"

"Yes," agreed Joe. "Sally thought it might be pleasant."

"It's terribly dry and arid here," said Miss Ross sadly. "That's the only body of water in a hundred miles or more. I hope it's pretty there. I've never seen it."

She handed Joe back his original memo from the facsimile machine. An exact copy of his written list, in his handwriting, was now in existence more than fifteen hundred miles away, and would arrive at the Kenmore Precision Tool plant within a matter of hours. There could be no question of errors in transmission! It had to be right!

Sally came out, smiled at her father's secretary, and led Joe down to the entrance.

80

"I have the car," she said cheerfully, "and there'll be a lunch basket waiting for us at the house. I agreed that the lake was too cold for swimming, though. It is. Snow water feeds it. But it's nice to look at."

They went out the door, and the workers on the Platform were just beginning to pile into the waiting fleet of busses. But the black car was waiting, too. Joe opened the door and Sally handed him the key. She regarded the men swarming on the busses.

"There'll be bulletins all over Bootstrap," she observed, "saying that Braun tried to dust-bomb the Shed. They'll say that he may have carried the cobalt about with him, and so he may have burned other people—in a restaurant, a movie theater, anywhere—while he was carrying the dust and dying without knowing it. So everybody's supposed to report to the hospital for a check-up for radiation burns. Some people may really have them. But Dad thinks that since you weren't burned, Braun didn't carry it around. If anyone is burned, it'll be the person who brought the cobalt here to give him. And—well—he'll turn up because everybody does, and because he's burned he'll be asked plenty of questions."

Joe stepped on the starter. Then he pressed the accelerator and the car sped forward.

They stopped at the house in the officers'-quarters area on the other side of the Shed. Sally picked up the lunch basket that her father's housekeeper had packed on telephoned instructions. They drove away.

Red Canyon was eighty miles from the Shed, and the only way to get there was through Bootstrap, because the only highway away from the Shed led to that small, synthetic town. It was irritating, though they had no schedule, to find that the long line of busses was ahead of them on that twenty-mile stretch. The busses ran nose to tail and filled the road for a half-mile or more. It was not possible to pass so long a string of close-packed vehicles. There was just enough traffic in the opposite direction to make that impracticable.

They had to trail the line of busses as far as Bootstrap and crawl through the crowded streets. Once beyond the town they came to a security stop. Here Sally's pass was good. Then they went rolling on and on through an empty, arid, sun-baked terrain toward the hills to the west. It looked remarkably lonely. Joe thought for the first time about gas. He looked carefully at the fuel gauge. Sally shook her head.

"Don't worry. Plenty of gas. Security takes care of that. When I said where we were going and that I wanted the car, Dad had everything checked. If I live through this, I'll bet I stay a fanatic about cautiousness all my life!"

Joe said distastefully: "I suppose it gets everybody. Mike—the midget, you know—called me back just now to suggest that the people who tried to spoil the gyros might try to harm the four of us to hinder their repair!"

"It's not just foolishness," Sally admitted. "The strain is pretty bad, especially when you know things. You've noticed that Dad's getting gray. That's strain. And Miss Ross is about as tense. Things leak out in the most remarkable way—and Dad can't find out how. Once there was a case of sabotage and he could have sworn that nobody had the information that permitted it but himself and Miss Ross. She had hysterics. She insisted that she wanted to be locked up somewhere so she couldn't be suspected of telling anybody anything. She'd resign tomorrow if she could. It's ghastly." Then she hesitated and smiled faintly: "In fact, so Dad wouldn't worry about me this afternoon— —"

He took his eyes off the road to glance at her.

"What?"

"I promised we wouldn't go swimming and— —" Then she said awkwardly: "There are two pistols in the glove compartment. Dad knows you. So I promised you'd put one in your pocket up at the lake."

Joe drew a deep breath. She opened the glove compartment and handed him a pistol. He looked at it: .38, hammerless. A good safe weapon. He slipped it in his coat pocket. But he frowned.

"I was looking forward to—not worrying for a while," he said wryly. "But now I'll have to remember to keep looking over my shoulder all the time!"

"Maybe," said Sally, "you can look over my shoulder and I'll look over yours, and we can glance at each other occasionally."

She laughed, and he managed to smile. But the trace of a frown remained on his forehead.

Joe drove and drove and drove. Once they came to a very small town. It may have contained a hundred people. There were gas pumps and a restaurant and two or three general stores, which were certainly too many for the permanent residents. But there were cow ponies hitched before the stores, and automobiles were also in view. The ground here was slightly rolling. The mountains had grown to good-sized ramparts against the sky. Joe drove carefully down the single street, turning out widely once to dodge a dog sleeping placidly in an area normally reserved for traffic.

Finally they came to the foothills, and then the road curved and recurved as it wound among them. And two hours from Bootstrap they reached Red Canyon. They first saw the dam from downstream. It was a monstrous structure of masonry, alone in the mountains. From its top a plume of falling water jetted out.

"The dam's for irrigation," said Sally professionally, "and the Shed gets all its power from here. One of Dad's nightmares is that somebody may blow up this dam and leave Bootstrap and the Shed without power."

Joe said nothing. He drove on up the trail as it climbed the canyon wall in hairpin slants. It was ticklish driving. But then, quite suddenly, they reached the top of the canyon wall and the top of the dam and the level of the lake at once. Here there was a sheet of water that reached back among the barren hillsides for miles and miles. It twisted out of sight. There were small waves on its surface, and grass at its edge. There were young trees. The powerhouse was a small squat structure in the middle of the dam. Not a person was visible anywhere.

"Here we are," said Sally, when Joe stopped the car.

He got out and went around to open the door for her. But she was already stepping out with the lunch basket in her hand when he arrived. He reached for it, and she held on, and they moved companionably away from the car carrying the basket between them.

"There's a nice place," said Sally, pointing.

A small ridge of rock stretched out into the lake, and rose, and spread, and formed what was almost a miniature island some fifty feet across. There were some young trees on it. Sally and Joe climbed down the slope and out the rocky isthmus that connected it with the shore.

Sally let down the lunch box on a stone and laughed for no reason at all as the wind blew her hair. It was a cool wind from over the water. And Joe realized with a shock of surprise that the air felt different and smelled different when it blew over open water like this. Up to now he hadn't thought of the dryness of the air in Bootstrap and the Shed.

The lunch basket was tilted a little. Joe picked it up and settled it more solidly. Then he said: "Hungry?"

There was literally nothing on his mind at the moment but the luxurious, satisfied feeling of being off somewhere with grass and a lake and Sally, and a good part of the afternoon to throw away. It felt good. So he lifted the lid of the lunch basket.

There was a revolver there. It was the other one from the glove compartment of the car. Sally hadn't left it behind. Joe regarded it and said ironically: "Happy, carefree youth—that's us! Which are the ham sandwiches, Sally?"

CHAPTER 8

Nevertheless, the afternoon began splendidly. Joe dunked the bottled soft drinks in the lake to cool. Then he and Sally ate and talked and laughed. Joe, in particular, had more than the usual capacity for enjoyment today. He'd been through twenty-four hours of turmoil but now things began to look better. And there was the arrangement with Sally, which had a solid satisfactoriness about it. Sally was swell! If she'd been homely, Joe would have liked her just the same—to talk to and to be with. But she was pretty—and she was wearing his ring. She'd wrapped some string around the inside of the band to make it fit.

The only trouble was that Joe was occasionally conscious of the heavy weight in his right-hand coat pocket.

But they spent at least an hour in contented, satisfying, meaningless loafing that nobody can describe but that everybody likes to remember afterward. From time to time Joe looked ashore, when the weight in his pocket reminded him of danger.

But he didn't look often enough. He was pulling the chilled soft-drink bottles out of the lake when he saw a movement out of the corner of his eye. He whirled, his hand in his pocket....

It was the Chief, with Haney and Mike the midget. They were striding across the rocky small peninsula.

Haney called sharply: "Everything okay?"

"Sure!" said Joe. "Everything's fine! What's the matter?"

"Mike had a hunch," said the Chief. "And—uh—I remembered I worked on the job when this dam was built twelve-fifteen years ago." He looked about him. "It looked different then."

Then he caught Joe's eye and jerked his head almost imperceptibly to one side. Joe caught the signal.

"I'll see about some more soft drinks," he said. "Come help me fish up the bottles."

Sally smiled at the other two. She was already inspecting the lunch basket.

"We still have some sandwiches," she said hospitably, "and some cake."

Haney came forward awkwardly. Mike advanced toward her with something of truculence. Joe knew what was in his mind. If Sally treated him like a freak.... But Joe knew with deep satisfaction that she wouldn't. He went down to the water's edge.

"What's up, Chief?" he asked in a low tone.

"Mike hadda hunch," rumbled the Chief. "Somebody tried to smash the stuff you brought. They did. But we started gettin' set to mend it. So what would they do? Polish us off. If they were set to atom-dust the whole Shed an' everybody in it, they wouldn't stop at four more murders."

Joe fished for a pop bottle.

"Mike said something like that back at the Shed," he observed.

"Yeah. But you were the one who figured things out. You'd be first target. Haney and Mike and me—we'd be hard to knock off in a crowd in Bootstrap. But you and her headed off by y'selves. Mike figured you mightn't be safe. So we checked."

Joe brought up one bottle and then another.

"We're all right. Haven't seen a soul."

"Don't mean a soul hasn't seen you," growled the Chief. "A car left Bootstrap less than twenty minutes behind you. There were three guys in it. It's parked down below the dam, outa sight. We saw it. And when we came up, careful, we spotted three guys hidin' out behind the rocks yonder. They look to me like they're waiting for somebody to go strolling back from the shoreline, so's—uh—maybe folks out at the powerhouse can't see 'em. That'd be you and her, huh?"

Joe went cold. Not for himself. For Sally.

"There's nobody else around," said the Chief. "Who'd they be waiting for but you two? Suppose they got a chance to kill you. They'd take the car keys. They'd drop your two bodies somewheres Gawdknowswhere. There'd be considerable of a hunt for you two. Major Holt would be upset plenty. Security might get loosened up. There might be breaks for guys who wanted to do a little extra sabotage—besides maybe hamperin' the repairin' of the pilot gyros. Then they could try for Haney and Mike and me."

Joe said coldly: "I've got a pistol and so has Sally. Shall we take those pistols and go ask those three if they want to start something?"

The Chief snorted.

"Use sense! It's good you got the pistols, though. I snagged a twenty-two rifle from a shooting gallery. It was all I could get in a hurry. But go huntin' trouble? Fella, I want to see that Platform go up! I'll take care of things now. Good layout here. They got to come across the open to get near. Don't say anything to Sally. But we'll keep our eyes open."

Joe nodded. He carried the chilled, dripping bottles back to where Haney solemnly ate a sandwich, sitting crosslegged with his back to the lake and regarding the shore. The Chief dragged a .22 repeating rifle from inside his belt, where it had hung alongside his thigh. He casually strolled over to Mike and dropped the rifle.

"You said you felt like target practice," he remarked blandly. "Here's your armament. Any more sandwiches, ma'am?"

Sally smilingly passed him the last. She left the top of the basket open. The pistol that had been there was gone. Then Sally's eyes met Joe's and she was aware that his three friends had not come here merely to crash a picnic. But she took it in stride. It was an additional reason for Joe to approve of Sally.

"Me," said the Chief largely, "I'm goin' to swim. I haven't had any more water around me than a shower bath for so long that I crave to soak and splash. I'll go yonder and dunk myself."

He wandered off, taking bites from the sandwich as he went. He vanished. Haney leaned back against a sapling, his eyes roving about the shoreline and the rocks and brush behind it.

Mike was talking in his crackling, high-pitched voice.

"But just the same it's crazy! Fighting sabotage when we little guys could take over in a week and make sabotage just plain foolish! We could do the whole job while the saboteurs weren't looking!"

Sally said with interest: "Have you got the figures? Were they ever passed on?"

"I spent a month's pay once," said Mike sardonically, "hiring a math shark to go over them. He found one mistake. It raised the margin of what we could do!"

Sally answered: "Joe! Listen to this! Mike says he has the real answer to sabotage, and, in a way, to space travel! Listen!"

Joe dropped to the ground.

"Shoot it," he said.

He was grimly alert, just the same. There were men waiting for them to start back to the car. These saboteurs were armed, and they intended to murder Sally and himself. Joe's jaws clamped tautly shut at the grim ideas that came into his mind.

But Mike was beginning to speak.

"Forget about the Platform a minute," he said, standing up to gesticulate, because he was only three and a half feet high. "Just figure on a rocket straight to the moon. With old-style rockets they'd a' had to have a mass ratio of a hundred and twenty to one. You'd have to burn a hundred and twenty tons of old-style fuel to land one ton on the moon. Now it could be done with sixty, and when the Platform's up, that figure'll drop again! Okay! You're gonna land a man on the moon. He weighs two hundred pounds. He uses up twenty pounds of food and drink and oxygen a day. Give him grub and air for two months—twelve hundred pounds. A cabin seven feet high and ten feet across. Sixteen hundred pounds, counting insulation an' braces for strength. That makes a pay load of a ton an' a half, and you'd have to burn a hundred an' eighty tons of fuel—old-style—to take it to the moon, and another hundred an' twenty for every ton the rocket ship weighed. You might get a man to the moon with a twelve-hundred-ton rocket— maybe. That's with the old fuels. He'd get there, an' he'd live two months, an' then he'd die for lack of air. With the new fuels you'd need ninety tons of fuel to carry the guy there, and sixty more for every ton the ship weighed itself. Call it six hundred tons for the rocket to carry one man to the moon."

Sally nodded absorbedly.

"I've seen figures like that," she agreed.

"But take a guy like me!" said Mike the midget bitterly. "I weigh forty-five pounds, not two hundred! I use four pounds of food and air a day. A cabin for me to live in would be four feet high an' five across. Bein' smaller, it wouldn't need so much bracing. You could do it for two hundred pounds. Three hundred for grub

88

and air, fifty for me. Me on the moon supplied for two months would come to five-fifty pounds. Sixteen tons of fuel to get me to the moon direct! To carry the weight of the ship—it's smaller!—fifty tons maximum!"

"I—see...," said Sally, frowning.

He looked at her suspiciously, but there was no mockery in her face.

"It'd take a six-hundred-ton rocket to get a full-sized man to the moon," he said with sudden flippancy, "but a guy my size could do the same job of stranglin' in a fifty-ton job. Counting how much easier it'd be to get back, with atmosphere deceleration, I could make a trip, land, take observations, pick up mineral specimens, and get back—all in a sixty-ton rocket. That's just ten per cent of what it'd cost to take a full-sized man one way!"

He stamped his foot. Then he said coldly: "Haney, sittin' still you're a sittin' duck!"

The comment was just. Joe knew that Sally was on the lakeward side of this small island, and that there were impenetrable rocks between her and the mainland. But Haney sat crosslegged where he could watch the mainland, and he hadn't moved in a long while. If someone did intend to commit murder from a distance, Haney was offering a chance for a very fine target. He moved.

"Yeah!" said Mike with fine irony, reverting to his topic. "I could show you plenty of figures! There are other guys like me! We've got as much brains as full-sized people! If the big brass had figured on us small guys, they coulda made the Platform the size of a four-family house an' it'd ha' been up in the sky right now, with guys like me running it. Guys my size could man the ferry rockets bringin' up fuel for storage, and four of us could take a six-hundred-ton rocket an' slide out to Mars an' be back by springtime—next springtime!—with all the facts and the photographs to prove 'em! By golly— —"

Then he made a raging, helpless gesture.

"But that's just the big picture," he said bitterly. "Right now, right at this minute, we could make it easy to finish the Platform the way it's building in the Shed! There are ferry rockets building somewhere else. You know about them?"

89

Sally said apologetically: "Yes. I know there'll be smaller rocket ships going up to the Platform. They'll carry fuel and stores and exchanges for the crew. Yes, I know there are ferry rockets building."

"Those ferry rockets," said Mike sardonically, "carry four men, plus two replacements for the crew. They'll carry air for ten days. But put four of us small guys in a ferry rocket! We'd have air and grub for two months, almost! Pull out the pay load and put in a hydroponic garden and communicators and we'd be a Platform, right then! Send up another ferry rocket to join us, and it could bring guided missiles! The ferry rockets could be finished quicker than the Platform! Send up three ferry rockets with midgets as crews, an' we could weld 'em together and have a Space Platform in orbit and working—and what'd be the use of sabotaging the big Platform then? The job would be done! There'd be no sense sabotaging the big Platform because the little one could do anything the big one could! It'd be up there and working! But," he demanded bitterly, "do you think anybody'll do anything as sensible as that?"

His small features were twisted in angry rebellion. And he was quite right in all his reasoning. Mankind could have made the journey to the planets in a hurry, and it could have had its Space Platform in the sky much more quickly, if only it could have consented to be represented by people like Mike—who would have represented mankind very valiantly.

Sally said distressedly: "Oh, Mike, it's all true and I'm so sorry!"

And she meant it. Joe liked Sally especially right then, because she didn't patronize Mike, or try to reason him out of his heartbreak.

Then Haney said abruptly: "Somebody's spotted the Chief."

Joe mentally kicked himself. The Chief had said he was going to swim. Now—but only now—Joe looked to see what he was doing.

He was far out from shore, swimming unhurriedly to the powerhouse at the middle of the dam. He would reach it, and swing up the ladder that could just be seen going down the lake side of the dam's top, and he would explain the situation on shore.

A telephone call to Bootstrap would bring security men rushing at eighty miles an hour, and parachute troopers a good deal faster. But even before they arrived the Chief would lead the powerhouse crew ashore armed with the shotguns they kept for shooting waterfowl in and out of season.

The men on shore might or might not consider the Chief's swim to be proof that he knew their intentions. They were probably discussing the matter in some agitation right now. But they couldn't know that the party on the semi-island was armed.

Suddenly Mike said crisply: "We're goin' to have visitors."

He lay down carefully on the ground, fifteen feet uphill from Sally, where he could look over the ridge. He snuggled the .22 target rifle professionally to his shoulder. He drew a bead.

Three men very casually strolled out of the brushwood on the shore. They moved nonchalantly toward the strand of rocks that led out to the picnic spot. They looked like anybody else from Bootstrap. Casual, rough work clothing.... Haney bent down and picked up four good throwing stones. His expression was pained.

Joe said: "We've got pistols, Haney, and Sally's a good shot."

The men came on. Their manner was elaborately casual. Joe stepped up into view.

"No visitors!" he called. "We don't want company!"

One of the men held his hand to his ear, as if not understanding. They came on. They made no threatening gestures.

Then Joe took his hand out of his pocket, the pistol Sally'd given him gripped tightly.

"I mean that!" he said harshly. "Stand back!"

One of the three spoke sharply. On that instant three snub-nosed pistols appeared. Bullets whined as the men hurtled forward. The purpose was not so much murder at this moment as the demoralizing effect of bullets flying overhead while the three assassins got close enough to do their bloody job with precision.

A stone whizzed by Joe—Haney had thrown it—and the small target rifle in Mike's hands coughed twice. Joe held his fire. He had only six bullets and three targets to hit. With a familiar revolver he'd have started shooting now, but thirty yards is a long range with a strange pistol at a moving target.

One of the three killers stumbled and crashed to the ground. A second seemed suddenly to be grinning widely on one side of his face. A .22 bullet had slashed his cheek. The third ran head on into a rock thrown by Haney. It knocked the breath out of him and his pistol fell from his hand.

Joe fired deliberately at the widely grinning man and saw him spin around. Mike's target rifle spat again and the man Joe had hit wheeled and ran heavily, making incoherent yells. The one who'd tumbled scrambled to his feet and fled, hopping crazily, favoring one leg. Deserted, the third man turned and ran too, still doubled over and still gasping.

Mike's voice crackled. He was in a towering rage because of the way the target rifle shot. It threw high and to the right. The shooting gallery paid off in cigarettes for high scores—so the guns didn't shoot straight.

Until this moment Joe had been relatively calm, because he had something to do. But just then he heard Sally say "Oh!" in a queer voice. He whirled. Unknown to him, she had not been waiting under cover, but standing with her pistol out and ready. And her face was very white, and she was plucking at her hair. A strand came away in her fingers. A bullet had clipped it just above her shoulder.

Then Joe went sick ... weak ... trembling, and he disgraced himself by half-hysterically grabbing Sally and demanding to know if she was hurt, and raging at her for exposing herself to fire, while his throat tried to close and shut off his breath from horror.

There came loud pop-pop-popping noises. With the peculiar reverberation of sound over water, two motorcycles started from the powerhouse along the crest of the dam. They streaked for the shore carrying five men, one of whom was the Chief, with a red-checked tablecloth about his middle, brandishing a fire axe in default of other weapons.

The danger was over.

But the assassins couldn't be followed immediately. They still had at least two pistols. Eight men and a girl, counting Mike, with an armament of only two pistols, a .22 rifle, two shotguns and a fire axe were not a properly equipped posse to hunt down killers. Also by now it was close to sunset.

So the victors did the sensible thing. Joe and Sally and Haney and the Chief—his clothes retrieved—plus Mike headed back for Bootstrap. Joe and Sally rode in the Major's black car, and the other three in the jalopy they'd rented for the afternoon. On the way into the canyon below the dam, they stopped at the parked car their would-be assassins had come in. They removed its distributor and fan belt. The other men returned to the powerhouse with their shotguns and the fire axe, and telephoned to Bootstrap. The three gunmen who had planned murder became fugitives, with no means of transportation but their legs. They had a good many thousand square miles of territory to hide in, but it wasn't likely that they had food or any competence to find it in the wilds. Two were certainly hurt. With dogs and planes and organization, it should be possible to catch them handily, come morning.

So Joe and Sally drove back to Bootstrap with the other car following closely through all the miles that had to be covered in the dark. Halfway back, they met a grim search party in cars, heading for the dam to begin their man hunt in the morning. After that, Joe felt better. But his teeth still tended to chatter every time he thought of Sally's startled, scared expression as she pulled away a lock of her hair that had been severed by a bullet.

When they got back to the Shed, Major Holt looked tired and old. Sally explained breathlessly that her danger was her own fault. Joe'd thought she was safely under cover....

"It was my fault," said the Major detachedly. "I let you go away from the Shed. I do not blame Joe at all."

But he did not look kindly. Joe wet his lips, ready to agree that any disgrace he might be subjected to was justified, since he had caused Sally to be shot at.

"I blame myself a great deal, sir," he said grimly. "But I can promise I'll never take Sally away from safety again. Not until the Platform's up and there's no more reason for her to be in danger."

The Major said remotely: "I shall have to arrange for more than that. I shall put you in touch with your father by telephone. You will explain to him, in detail, exactly how the repair of your

93

apparatus is planned. I understand that the gyros can be duplicated more quickly by the method you have worked out?"

Joe said: "Yes, sir. The balancing of the gyros can, which was the longest single job. But anything can be made quicker the second time. The patterns for the castings are all made, and the bugs worked out of the production process."

"You will explain that to your father," said the Major heavily. "Your father's plant will begin to duplicate these—ah—pilot gyros at once. Meanwhile your—ah—work crew will start to repair the one that is here."

"Yes, sir."

"And," said the Major, "I am sending you to the pushpot airfield. I intend to scatter the targets the saboteurs might aim at. You are one of them. Your crew is another. From time to time you will confer with them and verify their work. If any of them should be—disposed of, you will be able to instruct others."

"It's really the other way about, sir," objected Joe. "The Chief and Haney are pretty good, and Mike's got brains——"

The Major moved impatiently.

"I am looking at this from a security standpoint," he said. "I am trying to make it plainly useless to attack the gyros again. Duplicates will be in production at your father's plant. There will be three men repairing the smashed ones. There will be another man in another place—and this will be you—who can instruct new workmen in the repair procedure if anything should happen. Thus there will have to be three separate successful coups if the pilot gyros are not to be ready when the Platform needs them. Saboteurs might try one. Possibly two. But I think they will look for another weak spot to attack."

Joe did not like the idea of being moved away. He wanted to be on the job repairing the device that was primarily his responsibility. Besides, he had a feeling about Sally. If she were in danger, he wanted to be on hand.

"About Sally, sir——"

"Sally," said the Major tiredly, "is going to have to restrict herself to the point where she'll feel that jail would be preferable. But she will see the need for it. She will be guarded a good deal

94

more carefully than before—and you may not know it, but she has been guarded rather well."

Joe saw Sally smiling ruefully at him. What the Major had said was unpleasant, but he was right. This was one of those arrangements that nobody likes, an irritating, uncomfortable, disappointing necessity. But such necessities are a part of every actual achievement. The difference between things that get done and things that don't get done is often merely the difference between patience and impatience with tedious details. This arrangement would mean that Joe couldn't see Sally very often. It would mean that the Chief and Haney and Mike would do the actual work of getting the gyros ready. It would take all the glamour out of Joe's contribution. These deprivations shouldn't be necessary. But they were.

"All right, sir," said Joe gloomily. "When do I go over to the field?"

"Right away," said the Major. "Tonight." Then he added detachedly: "Officially, the excuse for your presence there will be that you have been useful in uncovering sabotage methods. You have. After all, through you a number of planes that would have been blown up have now had their booby traps removed. I know you do not claim credit for the fact, but it is an excuse for keeping you where I want you to be for another reason entirely. So it will be assumed that you are at the pushpot field for counter-sabotage inspection."

The Major nodded dismissal with an indefinable air of irony, and Joe went unhappily out of his office. He telephoned his father at length. His father did not share Joe's disappointment at being removed to a place of safety. He undertook to begin the castings for an entire new set of pilot gyros at once.

A little later Sally came out of her father's office.

"I'm sorry, Joe!"

He grinned unhappily.

"So am I. I don't feel very heroic, but if this is what has to be done to get the Platform out of the Shed and on the way up—it's what has to be done. I suppose I can phone you?"

"You can," said Sally. "And you'd better!"

They had talked a long time that afternoon, very satisfyingly and without any cares at all. Neither could have remembered much of what had been said. It probably was not earth-shaking in importance. But now there seemed to be a very great deal of other similar conversation urgently needing to be gone through.

"I'll call you!" said Joe.

Then somebody approached to take him to the pushpot airfield. They separated very formally under the eyes of the impersonal security officer who would drive Joe to his destination.

It was a tedious journey through the darkness. This particular security officer was not companionable. He was one of those conscientious people who think that if they keep their mouths shut it will make up for their inability to keep their eyes open. Socially he treated Joe as if he were a highly suspect person. It could be guessed that he treated everybody that way.

Joe went to sleep in the car.

He was only half-awake when he arrived, and he didn't bother to rouse himself completely when he was shown to a cubbyhole in the officers' barracks. He went to bed, making a half-conscious note to buy himself some clothes—especially fresh linen—in the morning.

Then he knew nothing until he was awaked in the early morning by what sounded exactly like the crack of doom.

CHAPTER 9

It was not, however, the crack of doom. When Joe stared out the window by the head of his cot, he saw gray-red dawn breaking over the landing field. There were low, featureless structures silhouetted against the sunrise. As the crimson light grew brighter, Joe realized that the angular shapes were hangars. Improbable crane poles loomed above them. One was in motion, handling something he could not make out, but the noise that had awakened him was less, now. It seemed to circle overhead, and it had an angry, droning, buzzing quality that was not natural in any motor he had ever heard before.

Joe shivered, standing at the window. It was cold and dank in the dawn light at this altitude, but he wanted to know what that completely unbelievable roar had been. A crane beam by the hangars tilted down, slowly, and then lifted as if released of a great weight. The light was growing slowly brighter. Joe saw something on the ground. Rather, it was not quite on the ground. It rested on something on the ground.

Suddenly that unholy uproar began again. Something moved. It ran heavily out from the masking dark of the hangars. It picked up speed. It acquired a reasonable velocity—forty or fifty miles an hour. As it scuttled over the dimly lighted field, it made a din like all the boiler factories in the world and all the backfiring motors in creation trying to drown each other's noise out—and all of them being very successful.

It was a pushpot. Joe recognized it with incredulity. It was one of those utterly ungainly creations that were built around one half of the sidewall of the Shed. In shape, its upper part was like the top half of a loaf of bread. In motion, here, it rested on some sort of wheeled vehicle, and it was reared up like an indignant caterpillar, and a blue-white flame squirted out of its tail, with coy and frolicsome flirtings from side to side.

The pushpot lifted from the vehicle on which it rode, and the vehicle put on speed and got away from under it with frantic agility. The vehicle swerved to one side, and Joe stared with amazed eyes at the pushpot, some twenty feet aloft. It had a flat underside, and a topside that still looked to him like the rounded top half of a loaf of baker's bread. It hung in the air at an angle of about forty-five degrees, and it howled like a panic-stricken dragon—Joe was getting his metaphors mixed by this time—and it swung and wobbled and slowly gained altitude, and then suddenly it seemed to get the knack of what it was supposed to do. It started to circle around, and then it began abruptly to climb skyward. Until it began to climb it looked heavy and clumsy and wholly unimpressive. But when it climbed, it really moved!

Joe found his head out the window, craning up to look at it. Its unearthly din took on the indignant quality of an irritated beehive. But it climbed! It went up without grace but with astonishing speed. And it was huge, but it became lost in the red-flecked dawn sky while Joe still gaped.

Joe flung on his clothes. He went out the door through resonant empty corridors, hunting for somebody to tell him something. He blundered into a mess hall. There were many tables, but the chairs around them were pushed back as if used and then left behind by people in a hurry to be somewhere else. There were exactly two people still visible over in a corner.

Another din like the wailing of a baby volcano with a toothache. It began, and moved, and went through the series of changes that ended in a climbing, droning hum. Another. Another. The launching of pushpots for their morning flight was evidently getting well under way.

Joe hesitated in the nearly empty mess hall. Then he recognized the two seated figures. They were the pilot and co-pilot, respectively, of the fateful plane that had brought him to Bootstrap.

He went over to their table. The pilot nodded matter-of-factly. The co-pilot grinned. Both still wore bandages on their hands, which would account for their remaining here.

"Fancy seeing you!" said the co-pilot cheerfully. "Welcome to the Hotel de Gink! But don't tell me you're going to fly a pushpot!"

"I hadn't figured on it," admitted Joe. "Are you?"

"Perish forbid," said the co-pilot amiably. "I tried it once, for the devil of it. Those things fly with the grace of a lady elephant on ice skates! Did you, by any chance, notice that they haven't got any wings? And did you notice where their control surfaces were?"

Joe shook his head. He saw the remnants of ham and eggs and coffee. He was hungry.

There was the uproar to be expected of a basso-profundo banshee in pain. Another pushpot was taking off.

"How do I get breakfast?" he asked.

The co-pilot pointed to a chair. He rapped sharply on a drinking glass. A door opened, he pointed at Joe, and the door closed.

"Breakfast coming up," said the co-pilot. "Look! I know you're Joe Kenmore. I'm Brick Talley and this is Captain—no less than Captain!—Thomas J. Walton. Impressed?"

"Very much," said Joe. He sat down. "What about the control surfaces on pushpots?"

"They're in the jet blast!" said the co-pilot, now identified as Brick Talley. "Like the V Two rockets when the Germans made 'em. Vanes in the exhaust blast, no kidding! Landing, and skidding in on their tails like they do, they haven't speed enough to give wing flaps a grip on the air, even if they had wings to put wing flaps on. Those dinkuses are things to have bad dreams about!"

Again, a door opened and a man in uniform with an apron in front came marching in with a tray. There was tomato juice and ham and eggs and coffee. He served Joe briskly and marched out again.

"That's Hotel de Gink service," said Talley. "No wasted motion, no sloppy civilities. He was about to eat that himself, he gave it to you, and now he'll cook himself a double portion of everything. What are you doing here, anyhow?"

Joe shrugged. It occurred to him that it would neither be wise nor creditable to say that he'd been sent here to split up a target at which saboteurs might shoot.

"I guess I'm attached for rations," he observed. "There'll be orders along about me presently, I suppose. Then I'll know what it's all about."

He fell to on his breakfast. The thunderous noises of the pushpots taking off made the mess hall quiver. Joe said between mouthfuls: "Funny way for anything to take off, riding on—it looked like a truck."

"It is a truck," said Talley. "A high-speed truck. Fifty of them specially made to serve as undercarriages so pushpot pilots can practice. The pushpots are really only expected to work once, you know."

Joe nodded.

"They aren't to take off," Talley explained. "Not in theory. They hang on to the Platform and heave. They go up with it, pushing. When they get it as high as they can, they'll shoot their jatos, let go, and come bumbling back home. So they have to practice getting back home and landing. For practicing it doesn't matter how they get aloft. When they get down, a big straddle truck on caterpillar treads picks them up—they land in the doggonedest places, sometimes!—and brings 'em back. Then a crane heaves them up on a high-speed truck and they do it all over again."

Joe considered while he ate. It made sense. The function of the pushpots was to serve as the first booster stage of a multiple-stage rocket. Together, they would lift the Platform off the ground and get it as high as their jet motors would take it traveling east at the topmost speed they could manage. Then they'd fire their jatos simultaneously, and in doing that they'd be acting as the second booster stage of a multiple-stage rocket. Then their work would be done, and their only remaining purpose would be to get their pilots back to the ground alive, while the Platform on its own third stage shot out to space.

"So," said Talley, "since their pilots need to practice landings, the trucks get them off the ground. They go up to fifty thousand feet, just to give their oxygen tanks a chance to conk out on them; then they barge around up there a while. The advanced trainees shoot off a jato at top speed. It's gauged to build them up to the speed they'll give the Platform. And then if they come out of that and get back down to ground safely, they uncross their fingers. A merry life those guys lead! When a man's made ten complete flights he retires. One flight a week thereafter to keep in practice only, until the big day for the Platform's take-off. Those guys sweat!"

"Is it that bad?"

100

The pilot grunted. The co-pilot—Talley—spread out his hands.

"It is that bad! Every so often one of them comes down untidily. There's something the matter with the motors. They've got a little too much power, maybe. Sometimes—occasionally—they explode."

"Jet motors?" asked Joe. "Explode? That's news!"

"A strictly special feature," said Talley drily. "Exclusive with pushpots for the Platform. They run 'em and run 'em and run 'em, on test. Nothing happens. But occasionally one blows up in flight. Once it happened warming up. That was a mess! The field's been losing two pilots a week. Lately more."

"It doesn't sound exactly reasonable," said Joe slowly. He put a last forkful in his mouth.

"It's also inconvenient," said Talley, "for the pilots."

The pilot—Walton—opened his mouth.

"It'd be sabotage," he said curtly, "if there was any way to do it. Four pilots killed this week."

He lapsed into silence again.

Joe considered. He frowned.

A pushpot, outside the building, hysterically bellowed its way across the runway and its noise changed and it was aloft. It went spiraling up and up. Joe stirred his coffee.

There were thin shoutings outside. A screaming, whistling noise! A crash! Something metallic shrieked and died. Then silence.

Talley, the co-pilot, looked sick. Then he said: "Correction. It's been five pushpots exploded and five pilots killed this week. It's getting a little bit serious." He looked sharply at Joe. "Better drink your coffee before you go look. You won't want to, afterward."

He was right.

Joe saw the crashed pushpot half an hour later. He found that his ostensible assignment to the airfield for the investigation of sabotage was quaintly taken at face value there. A young lieutenant solemnly escorted him to the spot where the pushpot had landed, only ten feet from a hangar wall. The impact had carried parts of the pushpot five feet into the soil, and the splash effect had caved in the hangar wall-footing. There'd been a fire, which had been put out.

101

The ungainly flying thing was twisted and torn. Entrails of steel tubing were revealed. The plastic cockpit cover was shattered. There were only grisly stains where the pilot had been.

The motor had exploded. The jet motor. And jet motors do not explode. But this one had. It had burst from within, and the turbine vanes of the compressor section were revealed, twisted intolerably where the barrel of the motor was ripped away. The jagged edges of the tear testified to the violence of the internal explosion.

Joe looked wise and felt ill. The young lieutenant very politely looked away as Joe's face showed how he felt. But of course there were the orders that said he was a sabotage expert. And Joe felt angrily that he was sailing under false colors. He didn't know anything about sabotage. He believed that he was probably the least qualified of anybody that security had ever empowered to look into methods of destruction.

Yet, in a sense, that very fact was an advantage. A man may be set to work to contrive methods of sabotage. Another man may be trained to counter him. The training of the second man is essentially a study of how the first man's mind works. Then it can be guessed what this saboteur will think and do. But such a trained security man will often be badly handicapped if he comes upon the sabotage methods of a second man—an entirely different saboteur who thinks in a new fashion. The security man may be hampered in dealing with the second man's sabotage just because he knows too much about the thinking of the first.

Joe went off and scowled at a wall, while the young lieutenant waited hopefully nearby.

He was in a false position. But he could see that there was something odd here. There was a sort of pattern in the way the other sabotage incidents had been planned. It was hard to pick out, but it was there. Joe thought of the trick of booby-trapping a plane during its major overhaul, and then arming the traps at a later date.... A private plane had been fitted to deliver proximity rockets in mid-air when the transport ship flew past. There was the explosion of the cargo parcel which was supposed to contain requisition forms and stationery. And the attempt to smash the entire Platform by getting an atomic bomb into a plane and having a saboteur shoot the crew and then deliver the bomb at the Shed in an officially harmless aircraft....

The common element in all those sabotage tricks was actually clear enough, but Joe wasn't used to thinking in such terms. He did know, though, that there was a pattern in those devices which did not exist in the blowing up of jet motors from inside.

He scowled and scowled, racking his brains, while the young lieutenant watched respectfully, waiting for Joe to have an inspiration. Had Joe known it, the lieutenant was deeply impressed by his attempt at concentration on the problem it had not been Major Holt's intention for Joe to consider. When Joe temporarily gave up, the young lieutenant eagerly showed him over the whole field and all its workings.

In mid-morning another pushpot fell screaming from the skies. That made six pushpots and six pilots for this week—two today. The things had no wings. They had no gliding angle. Pointed up, they could climb unbelievably. While their engines functioned, they could be controlled after a fashion. But they were not aircraft in any ordinary meaning of the word. They were engines with fuel tanks and controls in their exhaust blast. When their engines failed, they were so much junk falling out of the sky.

Joe happened to see the second crash, and he didn't go to noon mess at all. He hadn't any appetite. Instead, he gloomily let himself be packed full of irrelevant information by the young lieutenant who considered that since Joe had been sent by security to look into sabotage, he must be given every possible opportunity to evaluate—that would be the word the young lieutenant would use—the situation.

But all the time that Joe followed him about, his mind fumbled with a hunch. The idea was that there was a pattern of thinking in sabotage, and if you could solve it, you could outguess the saboteur. But the trouble was to figure out the similarity he felt existed in—say—a private plane shooting rockets and overhaul mechanics planting booby traps and faked shippers getting bombs on planes—and come to think of it, there was Braun....

Braun was the key! Braun had been an honest man, with an honest loyalty to the United States which had given him refuge. But

103

he had been blackmailed into accepting a container of atomic death to be released in the Shed. Radioactive cobalt did not belong in the Shed. That was the key to the pattern of sabotage. Braun was not to use any natural thing that belonged in the Shed. He was to be only the means by which something extraneous and deadly was to have been introduced.

That was it! Somebody was devising ingenious ways to get well-known destructive devices into places where they did not belong, but where they would be effective. Rockets. Bombs. Even radioactive cobalt dust. All were perfectly well-known means of destruction. The minds that planned those tricks said, in effect: "These things will destroy. How can we get them to where they will destroy something?" It was a strict pattern.

But the pushpot sabotage—and Joe was sure it was nothing else—was not that sort of thing. Making motors explode.... Motors don't explode. One couldn't put bombs in them. There wasn't room. The explosions Joe had seen looked as if they'd centered in the fire basket—technically the combustion area—behind the compressor and before the drive vanes. A jet motor whirled. Its front vanes compressed air, and a flame burned furiously in the compressed air, which swelled enormously and poured out past other vanes that took power from it to drive the compressor. The excess of blast poured out astern in a blue-white flame, driving the ship.

But one couldn't put a bomb in a fire basket. The temperature would melt anything but the refractory alloys of which a jet motor has to be built. A bomb placed there would explode the instant a motor was started. It couldn't resist until the pushpot took off. It couldn't....

This was a different kind of sabotage. There was a different mind at work.

In the afternoon Joe watched the landings, while the young lieutenant followed him patiently about. A pushpot landing was quite unlike the landing of any other air-borne thing. It came flying down with incredible clumsiness, making an uproar out of all proportion to its landing speed. Pushpots came in with their tail ends low, crudely and cruelly clumsy in their handling. They had

104

no wings or fins. They had to be balanced by their jet blasts. They had to be steered the same way. When a jet motor conked out there was no control. The pushpot fell.

He carefully watched one landing now. It came down low, and swung in toward the field, and seemed to reach its stern down tentatively to slide on the earth, and the flame of its exhaust scorched the field, and it hesitated, pointing up at an ever steeper angle—and it touched and its nose tilted forward—and leaped up as the jet roared more loudly, and then touched again....

The goal was for pushpots to touch ground finally with the whole weight of the flying monstrosity supported by the vertical thrust of the jet, and while it was moving forward at the lowest possible rate of speed. When that goal was achieved, they flopped solidly flat, slid a few feet on their metal bellies, and lay still. Some hit hard and tried to dig into the earth with their blunt noses. Joe finally saw one touch with no forward speed at all. It seemed to try to settle down vertically, as a rocket takes off. That one fell over backward and wallowed with its belly plates in the air before it rolled over on its side and rocked there.

The last of a flight touched down and flopped, and the memory of the wreckage had been overlaid by these other sights and Joe could think of his next meal without aversion. When it was evening-mess time he went doggedly back to the mess hall. There was a sort of itchy feeling in his mind. He knew something he didn't know he knew. There was something in his memory that he couldn't recall.

Talley and Walton were again at mess. Joe went to their table. Talley looked at him inquiringly.

"Yes, I saw both crashes," said Joe gloomily, "and I didn't want any lunch. It was sabotage, though. Only it was different in kind—it was different in principle—from the other tricks. But I can't figure out what it is!"

"Mmmmmm," said Talley, amiably. "You'd learn something if you could talk to the Resistance fighters and saboteurs in Europe. The Poles were wonderful at it! They had one chap who could get at the tank cars that took aviation gasoline from the refinery to the various Nazi airfields. He used to dump some chemical compound—just a tiny bit—into each carload of gas. It looked all right, smelled all right, and worked all right. But at odd moments Hitler's planes would crash. The valves would stick and the engine'd conk out."

Joe stared at him. And it was just as simple as that. He saw.

"The Nazis lost a lot of planes that way," said Talley. "Those that didn't crash from stuck valves in flight—they had to have their valves reground. Lost flying time. Wonderful! And when the Nazis did uncover the trick, they had to re-refine every drop of aviation gas they had!"

Joe said: "That's it!"

"That's it? And it is what?"

Then Joe said disgustedly: "Surely! It's the trick of loading CO_2 bottles with explosive gas, too! Excuse me!"

He got up from the table and hurried out. He found a phone booth and got the Shed, and then the security office, and at long last Major Holt. The Major's tone was curt.

"Yes?... Joe?... The three men from the affair of the lake were tracked this morning. When they were cornered they tried to fight. I am afraid we'll get no information from them, if that's what you wanted to know."

The Major's manner seemed to disapprove of Joe as expressing curiosity. His words meant, of course, that the three would-be murderers had been fatally shot.

Joe said carefully: "That wasn't what I called about, sir. I think I've found out something about the pushpots. How they're made to crash. But my hunch needs to be checked."

The Major said briefly: "Tell me."

Joe said: "All the tricks but one, that were used on the plane I came on, were the same kind of trick. They were all arrangements for getting regular destructive items—bombs or rockets or whatever—where they could explode and smash things. The saboteurs were adding destructive items to various states of things. But there was one trick that was different."

"Yes?" said the Major, on the telephone.

"Putting explosive gas in the CO_2 bottles," said Joe painstakingly, "wasn't adding a new gadget to a situation. It was

106

changing something that was already there. The saboteurs took something that belonged in a plane and changed it. They did not put something new into a plane—or a situation—that didn't belong there. It was a special kind of thinking. You see, sir?"

The Major, to do him justice, had the gift of listening. He waited.

"The pushpots," said Joe, very carefully, "naturally have their fuel stored in different tanks in different places, as airplanes do. The pilots switch on one tank or another just like plane pilots. In the underground storage and fueling pits, where all the fuel for the pushpots is kept in bulk, there are different tanks too. Naturally! At the fuel pump, the attendant can draw on any of those underground tanks he chooses."

The Major said curtly: "Obviously! What of it?"

"The pushpot motors explode," said Joe. "And they shouldn't. No bomb could be gotten into them without going off the instant they started, and they don't blow that way. I make a guess, sir, that one of the underground storage tanks—just one—contains doctored fuel. I'm guessing that as separate tanks in a pushpot are filled up, one by one, one is filled from a particular underground storage tank that contains doctored fuel. The rest will have normal fuel. And the pushpot is going to crash when that tank, and only that tank, is used!"

Major Holt was very silent.

"You see, sir?" said Joe uneasily. "The pushpots could be fueled a hundred times over with perfectly good fuel, and then one tank in one of them would explode when drawn on. There'd be no pattern in the explosions...."

Major Holt said coldly: "Of course I see! It would need only one tank of doctored fuel to be delivered to the airfield, and it need not be used for weeks. And there would be no trace in the wreckage, after the fire! You are telling me there is one underground storage tank in which the fuel is highly explosive. It is plausible. I will have it checked immediately."

He hung up, and Joe went back to his meal. He felt uneasy. There couldn't be any way to make a jet motor explode unless you fed it explosive fuel. Then there couldn't be any way to stop it. And then—after the wreck had burned—there couldn't be any way to prove it was really sabotage. But the feeling of having reported only a guess was not too satisfying. Joe ate gloomily. He didn't pay much attention to Talley. He had that dogged, uncomfortable feeling a man has when he knows he doesn't qualify as an expert, but feels that he's hit on something the experts have missed.

Half an hour after the evening mess—near sunset—a security officer wearing a uniform hunted up Joe at the airfield.

"Major Holt sent me over to bring you back to the Shed," he said politely.

"If you don't mind," said Joe with equal politeness, "I'll check that."

He went to the phone booth in the barracks. He got Major Holt on the wire. And Major Holt hadn't sent anybody to get him.

So Joe stayed in the telephone booth—on orders—while the Major did some fast telephoning. It was comforting to know he had a pistol in his pocket, and it was frustrating not to be allowed to try to capture the fake security officer himself. The idea of murdering Joe had not been given up, and he'd have liked to take part personally in protecting himself. But it was much more important for the fake security man to be captured than for Joe to have the satisfaction of attempting it himself.

As a matter of fact, the fake officer started his getaway the instant Joe went to check on his orders. The officer knew they'd be found faked. It had not been practical for him to shoot Joe down where he was. There were too many people around for this murderer to have a chance at a getaway.

But he didn't get away, at that. Twenty minutes later, while Joe still waited fretfully in the phone booth, the phone bell rang and Major Holt was again on the wire. And this time Joe was instructed to come back to the Shed. He had exact orders whom to come with, and they had orders which identified them to Joe.

Some eight miles from the airfield—it was just dusk—Joe came upon a wrecked car with motorcycle security guards working on it. They stopped Joe's escort. Joe's phone call had set off an alarm. A plane had spotted this car tearing away from the airfield, and motorcyclists were guided in pursuit by the plane. When it

108

wouldn't stop—when the fake Security officer in it tried to shoot his way clear—the plane strafed him. So he was dead and his car was a wreck, and the motorcycle men were trying to get some useful information from his body and the car.

Joe went to the Major's house in the officers'-quarters area. The Major looked even more tired than before, but he nodded approvingly at Joe. Sally was there too, and she regarded Joe with a look which was a good deal warmer than her father's.

"You did very well," said the Major detachedly. "I don't have too high an opinion of the brains of anybody your age, Joe. When you are my age, you won't either. But whether you have brains or simply luck, you are turning out to be very useful."

Joe said: "I'm getting security conscious, sir. I want to stay alive."

The Major regarded him with irony.

"I was thinking of the fact that when you worked out the matter of the doctored pushpot fuel, you did not try to be a hero and prove it yourself. You referred it to me. That was the proper procedure. You could have been killed, investigating—it's clear that the saboteurs would be pleased to have a good chance to murder you—and your suspicions might never have reached me. They were correct, by the way. One storage tank underground was half-full of doctored fuel. Rather more important, another was full, not yet drawn on."

The Major went on, without apparent cordiality: "It seems probable that if this particular sabotage trick had not been detected—it seems likely that on the Platform's take-off, all or most of the pushpots would have been fueled to explode at some time after the Platform was aloft, and before it could possibly get out to space."

Joe felt queer. The Major was telling him, in effect, that he might have kept the Platform from crashing on take-off. It was a good but upsetting sensation. It was still more important to Joe that the Platform get out to space than that he be credited with saving it. And it was not reassuring to hear that it might have been wrecked.

"Your reasoning," added the Major coldly, "was soundly based. It seems certain that there is not one central authority directing all the sabotage against the Platform. There are probably several sabotage organizations, all acting independently and probably hating each other, but all hating the Platform more."

Joe blinked. He hadn't thought of that. It was disheartening.

"It will really be bad," said the Major, "if they ever co-operate!"

"Yes, sir," said Joe.

"But I called you back from the airfield," the Major told him without warmth, "to say that you have done a good job. I have talked to Washington. Naturally, you deserve a reward."

"I'm doing all right, sir," said Joe awkwardly. "I want to see the Platform go up and stay up!"

The Major nodded impatiently.

"Naturally! But—ah—one of the men selected and trained for the crew of the Platform has been—ah—taken ill. In strict confidence, because of sabotage it has been determined to close in the Platform and get it aloft at the earliest possible instant, even if its interior arrangements are incomplete. So—ah—in view of your usefulness, I said to Washington that I believed the greatest reward you could be offered was—ah—to be trained as an alternate crew member, to take this man's place if he does not recover in time."

The room seemed to reel around Joe. Then he gulped and said: "Yes, sir! I mean—that's right. I mean, I'd rather have that, than all the money in the world!"

"Very well." The Major turned to leave the room. "You'll stay here, be guarded a good deal more closely than before, and take instructions. But you understand that you are still only an alternate for a crew member! The odds are definitely against your going!"

"That's—that's all right, sir," said Joe unsteadily. "That's quite all right!"

The Major went out. Joe stood still, trying to realize what all this might mean to him. Then Sally stirred.

"You might say thanks, Joe."

Her eyes were shining, but she looked proud, too.

"I put it in Dad's head that that was what you'd like better than anything else," she told him. "If I can't go up in the Platform myself—and I can't—I wanted you to. Because I knew you wanted to."

110

She smiled at him as he tried incoherently to talk. With a quiet maternal patience, she led him out on the porch of her father's house and sat there and listened to him. It was a long time before he realized that she was humoring him. Then he stopped short and looked at her suspiciously. He found that in his enthusiastic gesticulations he had been gesticulating with her hand as well as his own.

"I guess I'm pretty crazy," he said ruefully. "Shooting off my mouth about myself up there in space.... You're pretty decent to stand me the way I am, Sally."

He paused. Then he said humbly: "I'm plain lucky. But knowing you and—having you like me reasonably much is pretty lucky too!"

She looked at him noncommittally.

He added painfully: "And not only because you spoke to your father and told him just the right thing, either. You're—sort of swell, Sally!"

She let out her breath. Then she grinned at him.

"That's the difference between us, Joe," she told him. "To me, what you just said is the most important thing anybody's said tonight."

CHAPTER 10

The world turned over on its axis with unfailing regularity, and nights followed mornings and mornings followed nights according to well-established precedent. One man turned up in Bootstrap with radiation burns, but he had not offered himself for check over at the hospital. He was found dead in his lodging. Since nobody else appeared to have suffered any burns at all, it was assumed that he was the messenger who had brought the radioactive cobalt to Braun, who also had been doomed by possession of the deadly stuff, but who had broken the chain of fatality by not dumping it free into the air of the Shed. Under the circumstances, then, three-shift work on the Platform was resumed, and three times in each twenty-four hours fleets of busses rolled out of Bootstrap carrying men to work in the Shed, and rolled back again loaded with men who had just stopped working there.

Trucks carried materials to the Shed, and swing-up doors opened in the great dome's eastern wall, and the trucks went in and unloaded. Then the trucks went out of the same doors and trundled back for more materials. In the Shed, shining plates of metal swung aloft, and welding torches glittered in the maze of joists and upright pipes that still covered the monster shape. Each day it was a little more nearly complete. In a separate, guarded workshop by a sidewall, the Chief and Haney and Mike the midget labored mightily to accomplish the preposterous. They grew lean and red-eyed from fatigue, and short of temper and ever more fanatical— and security men moved about in seeming uselessness but never-ceasing vigilance.

There were changes, though. The assembly line of pushpots grew shorter, and the remaining monstrosities around the sidewall were plainly near to completion. There came a day, indeed, when only five ungainly objects remained on that line, and even they were completely plated in and needed only a finishing touch. It was at this time that more crates and parcels arrived from the Kenmore Precision Tool plant, and Joe dropped his schoolroomlike instruction course in space flight for work of greater immediate

112

need. He and his allies worked twice around the clock to assemble the replaced parts with the repaired elements of the pilot gyros. They grew groggy from the desperate need both for speed and for absolute accuracy, but they put the complex device together, and adjusted it, and surveyed the result through red-rimmed eyes, and were too weary to rejoice.

Then Joe threw a switch and the reconstituted pilot gyro assembly began to hum quietly, and the humming rose to a whine, and the whine went deliberately up the scale until it ceased to be audible at all. Presently a dial announced the impossible, and they gazed at a device that seemed to be doing nothing whatever. The gyros appeared quite motionless. They spun with such incredible precision that it was not possible to detect that they moved a hairbreadth. And the whole complex device looked very simple and useless.

But the four of them gazed at it—now that it worked—with a sudden passionate satisfaction. Joe moved a control, and the axis of the device moved smoothly to a new place and stayed there. He moved the control again, and it moved to another position and stayed there. And to another and another and another.

Then the Chief took Joe's place, and under his hand the seemingly static disks—which were actually spinning at forty thousand revolutions per minute—turned obediently and without any appearance of the spectacular. Then Haney worked the controls. And Mike put the device through its paces.

Mike left the gyros spinning so that the main axis pointed at the sun, invisible beyond the Shed's roof. And then all four of them watched. It took minutes for this last small test to show its results. But visibly and inexorably the pilot gyros followed the unseen sun, and they would have resisted with a force of very many tons any attempt to move them aside by so little as one-tenth of a second of arc, which would mean something like one three-hundred-thousandth of a right angle. And these pilot gyros would control the main gyros with just this precision, and after the Platform was out in space could hold the Platform itself with the steadiness needed for astronomical observation past achievement from the surface of the Earth.

113

The pilot gyros, in a word, were ready for installation.

Joe and Haney and the Chief and Mike were not beautiful to look at. They were begrimed from head to toe, and their eyes were bloodshot, and they were exhausted to the point where they did not even notice any longer that they were weary. And their mental processes were not at all normal, so that they were quarrelsome and arbitrary and arrogant to the men with the flat-bed trailer who came almost reverently to move their work. They went jealously with the thing they had rebuilt, and they were rude to engineers and construction workers and supervisors, and they shouted angrily at each other as it was hoisted up a shaft that had been left in the Platform for its entrance, and they were very far from tactful as they watched with hot, anxious eyes as it was bolted into place.

It would be welded later, but first it was tried out. And it moved the main gyros! They weighed many times what the pilot gyros did, but even when they were spinning the pilot gyros stirred them. Of course the main-gyro linkage to the fabric of the Shed had to be broken for this test, or the gyros would have twisted the giant upon its support and all the scaffolding around it would have been broken and the men on it killed.

But the gyros worked! They visibly and unquestionably worked! They controlled the gigantic wheels that would steer the Platform in its take-off, and later would swing it to receive the cargo rockets coming up from Earth. The pilot instrument worked! There was no vibration. In its steering apparatus the Platform was ready for space!

Then the Chief yawned, and his eyes glazed as he stood in the huge gyro room. And Haney's knees wobbled, and he sat down and was instantly asleep. Then Joe vaguely saw somebody—it was Major Holt—holding Mike in his arms as if Mike were a baby. Mike would have resented it furiously if he had been awake. And then suddenly Joe didn't know what was going on around him, either.

There was a definite hiatus in his consciousness. He came back to awareness very slowly. He was half-awake and half-asleep for a long time. He only knew contentedly that his job was finished. Then, slowly, he realized that he was in a bunk in one of the Platform sleeping cabins, and the inflated cover that was Sally's

114

contribution to the Platform held him very gently in place. Somehow it was infinitely soothing, and he had an extraordinary sensation of peacefulness and relaxation and fulfillment. The pilot gyros were finished and in position. His responsibility to them was ended. And he had slept the clock around three times. He'd slept for thirty-six hours. He was starving.

Sally had evidently constituted herself a watch over Joe as he slept, because she faced him immediately when he went groggily out of the cabin to look for a place to wash. He was still covered with the grime of past labor, and he had been allowed to sleep with only his shoes removed. He was not an attractive sight. But Sally regarded him with an approval that her tone belied.

"You can get a shower," she told him firmly, "and then I'll have some breakfast for you. Fresh clothes are waiting, too."

Joe said peacefully: "The gyros are finished and they work!"

"Don't I know?" demanded Sally. "Go get washed and come back for breakfast. The Chief and Haney and Mike are already awake. And because of the four of you, they've been able to advance the Platform's take-off time—to just two days off! It leaked out, and now it's official. And you made it possible!"

This was a slight exaggeration, but it was pardonable because of Sally's partiality for Joe. He went groggily into the special shower arrangement in the Platform. In orbit, there would be no gravity, so a tub bath was unthinkable. The shower cabinet was a cubbyhole with handgrips on all four sides and straps into which one could slip his feet. When Joe turned handles, needle sprays sprang at him from all sides, and simultaneously a ventilator fan began to run. When in space that fan could draw out what would otherwise become an inchoate mixture of air and quite weightless water-drops. In space a man might drown in his own shower bath without the fan. The apparatus for collecting the water again was complex, but Joe didn't think about that at the moment. He considered ruefully that however convenient this system might be out in the Platform's orbit, it left something to be desired on Earth.

But there were clean clothes waiting when he came out. He dressed and felt brand new and utterly peaceful and rested, and it seemed to him very much like the way he had often felt on a new spring morning. It was very, very good!

Then he smelled coffee and became ravenous.

There were the others in the Platform's kitchen, sitting in the chairs that had straps on them so the crew needn't float about because of weightlessness. There was an argument in progress. The Chief grinned at Joe. Mike the midget looked absorbed. Haney was thinking something out, rather painfully. Sally was busy at the Platform's very special stove. She had ham and eggs and pancakes ready for Joe to eat.

"Gentlemen," she said, "you are about to eat the first meal ever cooked in a space ship—and like it!"

She served them and sat companionably down with them all. But her eyes were very warm when she looked at Joe.

"Leavin' aside what we were arguin' about," said the Chief blissfully, "Sally here—mind if I call you Sally, ma'am?—she says the slide-rule guys have given our job the works and they say it's a better job than they designed. Take a bow, Joe."

Sally said firmly: "When the technical journals are through talking about the job you did, you'll all four be famous for precision-machining technique and improvements on standard practices."

"Which," said the Chief sarcastically, "is gonna make us feel fine when we're back to welding and stuff!"

"No more welding," Sally told him. "Not on this job. The Platform's closed in. They've started to take down the scaffolding."

The Chief looked startled. Haney asked: "Laying off men yet?"

"Not you," Sally assured him. "Definitely not you. You four have the very top super-special security rating there is! I think you're the only four people in the world my father is sure can't be reached, somehow, to make you harm the Platform."

Mike said abruptly: "Yeah. The Major thought he had headaches before. Now he's really got 'em!"

Mike hadn't seemed to be listening. He'd acted as if he were feverishly absorbing the feel of being inside the Platform—not as a workman building it, but as a man whose proper habitat it would become. But Joe suddenly realized that his comment was exact.

116

There'd been plenty of sabotage to prevent the Platform from reaching completion. But now it was ready to take off in two days. If it was to be stopped, it would have to be stopped within forty-eight hours by people with plenty of resources, who for their own evil ends needed it to be stopped. These last two days would contain the last-ditch, most desperate, most completely ruthless stepped-up attempts at destruction that could possibly be made. And Major Holt had to handle them.

But the four at table—five, with Sally—were peculiarly relaxed. The matter they'd handled had been conspicuous, perhaps, but it was still only one of thousands that had to be accomplished before the Platform could take off. But they had the infinitely restful feeling of a job well done.

"No more welding," said Haney meditatively, "and our job on the gyros finished. What are we gonna do?"

The Chief said forcefully: "Me, I'm gonna sweep floors or something, but I'm sure gonna stick around and watch the take-off!"

Joe said nothing. He looked at Sally. She became very busy, making certain the others did not want more to eat. After a long time Joe said, with very careful casualness, "Come to think of it, I was getting loaded up with astrogation theory when I had to stop and pitch in on the gyros. How's that sick crew member, Sally?"

"I—wouldn't know," answered Sally unconvincingly. "Have some more coffee?"

Joe made his face go completely expressionless. There was nothing else to do. Sally hadn't said that his chances looked bad for making the crew of the Platform when it went out to space. But Sally had ways of knowing things. She would be sure to keep informed on a matter like that, because she was wearing Joe's ring and it would have taken a great deal of discouragement to keep her from finding out good news to tell him. She didn't have any good news. So it must be bad.

Joe drank his coffee, trying to make himself believe that he'd known all along he wasn't going to make the crew. He'd started late to learn the things a crew member ought to know. He'd stopped at the most crucial part of his training to work on the

117

gyros, which were more crucial still. He'd slept a day and a half. The platform would take off in forty-eight hours. He tried to reason carefully that it was common sense to use a man who was fully trained from the beginning for a place in the crew, rather than a latecomer like himself. But it wasn't easy to take.

Mike the midget said suddenly: "I got a hunch."

"Shoot it," said the Chief, amiably.

"I got a hunch I know what kind of sabotage will be tried next—and when," said Mike.

The others looked at him—all but Joe, who stared at the wall.

"There hasn't been one set of guys trying to smash the Platform," said Mike excitedly. "There's been four or five. Joe found a gang sabotaging the pushpots that didn't think like the gang that blackmailed Braun. And the gang that tried to kill us up at Red Canyon may be another. There could be others: fascists and commies and nationalists and crackpots of all kinds. And they all know they've got to work fast, even if they have to help each other. Get it?"

Haney growled.

"I'll buy what you've said so far," said the Chief. "Sure! Those so-and-sos will all pile in everything they got at the last minute. They'll even pull together to smash the Platform—and then double-cross each other afterward. But what'll they do, an' when?"

"This time they'll try outright violence," said Mike coldly, "instead of sneaking. They'll try something really rough. For sneaking, one time's as good as another, but for really rough stuff, there's just one time when the Platform hasn't got plenty of guys around ready to fight for it."

The Chief whistled softly.

"You mean change-shift time! Which one?"

"The first one possible," said Mike briefly. "After every shift, things will get tighter. So my guess is the next shift, if they can. And if one gang starts something, the others will have to jump right in. You see?"

That made sense. One attempt at actual violence, defeated, would create a rigidity of defense that would make others impossible. If a successful attempt at violent sabotage was to be

118

made, the efforts of all groups would have to be timed to the first, or abandoned.

"I could—uh—set up a sort of smoke screen," said Mike. "We'll fake we're going to smash something—and let those saboteurs find it out. They'll see it as a chance to do their stuff with us to run interference for them.—Sally, does your father sure-enough trust us?"

Sally nodded.

"He doesn't talk very cordially, but he trusts you."

"Okay," said Mike. "You tell him, private, that I'm setting up something tricky. He can laugh off anything his security guys report that I'm mixed up in. Joe'll see that he gets the whole picture beforehand. But he ain't to tell anybody—not anybody—that something is getting framed up. Right?"

"I'll ask him," said Sally. "He is pretty desperate. He's sure some last-minute frantic assault on the Platform will be made. But——"

"We'll tip him in plenty of time," said Mike with authority. "In time for him to play along, but not for a leak to spoil things. Okay?"

"I'll make the bargain," Sally assured him, "if it can be made."

Mike nodded. He drained his coffee cup and slipped down from his chair.

"Come on, Chief! C'mon, Haney!"

He led them out of the room.

Joe fiddled with his spoon a moment, and then said: "The crewman I was to have subbed for if he didn't get well—he did, didn't he?"

Sally answered reluctantly: "Y-yes."

Joe said measuredly: "Well, then—that's that! I guess it will be all right for me to stick around and watch the take-off?"

Sally's eyes were misty.

"Of course it will, Joe! I'm so sorry!"

Joe grinned, but even to himself his face seemed like a mask.

"Into each life some rain must fall. Let's go out and see what's been accomplished since I went to sleep. All right?"

They went out of the Platform together. And as soon as they

reached the floor of the Shed it was plain that the stage had been set for stirring events.

The top five or six levels of scaffolding had already been removed, and more of the girders and pipes were coming down in bundles on lines from giraffelike cranes. There were some new-type trucks in view, too, giants of the kind that carry ready-mixed concrete through city streets. They were pouring a doughy white paste into huge buckets that carried it aloft, where it vanished into the mouths of tubes that seemed to replace the scaffolding along the Platform's sides.

"Lining the rockets," said Sally in a subdued voice.

Joe watched. He knew about this, too. It had been controversial for a time. After the pushpots and their jatos had served as the first two stages of a multiple-rocket aggregation, the Platform carried rocket fuel as the third stage. But the Platform was a highly special ballistic problem. It would take off almost horizontally—a great advantage in fueling matters. This was practical simply because the Platform could be lifted far beyond effective air resistance, and already have considerable speed before its own rockets flared.

Moreover, it was not a space ship in the sense of needing rockets for landing purposes. It wouldn't land. Not ever. And again there was the fact that men would be riding in it. That ruled out the use of eight- and ten- and fifteen-gravity acceleration. It had to make use of a long period of relatively slow acceleration rather than a brief terrific surge of power. So its very special rockets had been designed as the answer.

They were solid-fuel rockets, though solid fuels had been long abandoned for long-range missiles. But they were entirely unlike other solid-fuel drives. The pasty white compound being hauled aloft was a self-setting refractory compound with which the rocket tubes would be lined, with the solid fuel filling the center. The tubes themselves were thin steel—absurdly thin—but wound with wire under tension to provide strength against bursting, like old-fashioned rifle cannon.

When the fuel was fired, it would be at the muzzle end of the rocket tube, and the fuel would burn forward at so many inches per second. The refractory lining would resist the rocket blast for a

120

certain time and then crumble away. Crumbling, the refractory particles would be hurled astern and so serve as reaction mass. When the steel outer tubes were exposed, they would melt and be additional reaction mass.

In effect, as the rocket fuel was exhausted, the tubes that contained it dissolved into their own blast and added to the accelerating thrust, even as they diminished the amount of mass to be accelerated. Then the quantity of fuel burned could diminish— the tubes could grow smaller—so the rate of speed gain would remain constant. Under the highly special conditions of this particular occasion, there was a notable gain in efficiency over a liquid-fuel rocket design. For one item, the Platform would certainly have no use for fuel pumps and fuel tanks once it was in its orbit. In this way, it wouldn't have them. Their equivalent in mass would have been used to gain velocity. And when the Platform finally rode in space, it would have expended every ounce of the driving apparatus used to get it there.

Now the rocket tubes were being lined and loaded. The time to take-off was growing short indeed.

Joe watched a while and turned away. He felt very good because he'd finished his job and lived up to the responsibility he'd had. But he felt very bad because he'd had an outside chance to be one of the first men ever to make a real space journey—and now it was gone. He couldn't resent the decision against him. If it had been put up to him, he'd probably have made the same hard decision himself. But it hurt to have had even a crazy hope taken away.

Sally said, trying hard to interest him, "These rockets hold an awful lot of fuel, Joe! And it's better than scientists thought a chemical fuel could ever be!"

"Yes," said Joe.

"Fluorine-beryllium," said Sally urgently. "It fits in with the pushpots' having pressurized cockpits. Rockets like that couldn't be used on the ground! The fumes would be poisonous!"

But Joe only nodded in agreement. He was apathetic. He was uninterested. He was still thinking of that lost trip in space. He realized that Sally was watching his face.

"Joe," she said unhappily, "I wish you wouldn't look like that!"

"I'm all right," he told her.

"You act as if you didn't care about anything," she protested, "and you do!"

"I'm all right," he repeated.

"I'd like to go outside somewhere," she said abruptly, "but after what happened up at the lake, I mustn't. Would you like to go up to the top of the Shed?"

"If you want to," he agreed without enthusiasm.

He followed when she went to a doorway—with a security guard beside it—in the sidewall. She flashed her pass and the guard let them through. They began to walk up an inclined, endless, curving ramp. It was between the inner and outer skins of the Shed. There had to be two skins because the Shed was too big to be ventilated properly, and the hot desert sunshine on one side would have made "weather" inside. There'd have been a convection-current motion of the air in the enclosed space, and minor whirlwinds, and there could even be miniature thunderclouds and lightning. Joe remembered reading that such things had happened in a shed built for Zeppelins before he was born.

They came upon an open gallery, and there was a security man looking down at the floor and the Platform. He had a very good view of all that went on.

They went around another long circuit of the slanting gallery, dimly lighted with small electric bulbs. They came to a second gallery, and saw the Platform again. There was another guard here.

They were halfway up the globular wall now, and were visibly suspended over emptiness. The view of the Platform was impressive. There were an astonishing number of rocket tubes being fastened to the outside of that huge object. Three giant cranes, working together, hoisted a tube to the last remaining level of scaffolding, and men swarmed on it and fastened it to the swelling hull. As soon as it was fast, other men hurried into it with the white pasty stuff to line it from end to end. The tubes would nearly hide the structure they were designed to propel. But they'd all be burned away when it reached its destination.

"Wonderful, isn't it?" asked Sally hopefully.

122

Joe looked, and said without warmth, "It's the most wonderful thing that anybody ever even tried to do."

Which was true enough, but the zest of it had unreasonably departed for Joe for the time being. His disappointment was new.

Halfway around again, Sally opened a door, and Joe was almost surprised out of his lethargy. Here was a watching post on the outside of the monstrous half-globe. There were two guards here, with fifty-caliber machine guns under canvas hoods. Their duties were tedious but necessary. They watched the desert. From this height it stretched out for miles, and Bootstrap could be seen as a series of white specks far away with hills behind it.

Ultimately Sally and Joe came to the very top of the Shed into the open air. From here the steep plating curved down and away in every direction. The sunshine was savagely bright and shining, but there was a breeze. And here there was a considerable expanse fenced in—almost an acre, it seemed. There were metal-walled small buildings with innumerable antennae of every possible shape for the reception of every conceivable wave length. There were three radar bowl reflectors turning restlessly to scan the horizon, and a fourth which went back and forth, revolving, to scan the sky itself. Sally told Joe that in the very middle—where there was a shed with a domelike roof which wasn't metal—there was a wave-guide radar that could spot a plane within three feet vertically, and horizontally at a distance of thirty miles, with greater distances in proportion.

There were guns down in pits so their muzzles wouldn't interfere with the radar. There were enough non-recoil anti-aircraft guns to defend the Shed against anything one could imagine.

"And there are jet planes overhead too," said Sally. "Dad asked to have them reinforced, and two new wings of jet fighters landed yesterday at a field somewhere over yonder. There are plenty of guards!"

The Platform was guarded as no object in all history had ever been guarded. It was ironic that it had to be protected so, because it was actually the only hope of escape from atomic war. But that was why some people hated the Platform, and their hatred had made it seem obviously an item of national defense. Ironically that was the reason the money had been provided for its construction. But the greatest irony of all was that its most probable immediate usefulness would be the help it would give in making nuclear experiments that weren't safe enough to make on Earth.

That was pure irony. Because if those experiments were successful, they should mean that everybody in the world would in time become rich beyond envy.

But Joe couldn't react to the fact. He was drained and empty of emotion because his job was done and he'd lost a very flimsy hope to be one of the Platform's first crew.

He didn't really feel better until late that night, when suddenly he realized that life was real and life was earnest, because a panting man was trying to strangle Joe with his bare hands. Joe was hampered in his self-defense because a large number of battling figures trampled over him and his antagonist together. They were underneath the Platform, and Joe expected to be blown to bits any second.

CHAPTER 11

Joe sat on the porch of Major Holt's quarters in the area next to the Shed. It was about eight-thirty, and dark, but there was a moon. And Joe had come to realize that his personal disappointment was only his personal disappointment, and that he hadn't any right to make a nuisance of himself about it. Therefore he didn't talk about the thing nearest in his mind, but something else that was next nearest or farther away still. Yet, with the Shed filling up a full quarter of the sky, and a gibbous moon new-risen from the horizon, it was not natural for a young man like Joe to speak purely of earthly things.

"It'll come," he said yearningly, staring at the moon. "If the Platform gets up day after tomorrow, it's going to take time to ferry up the equipment it ought to have. But still, somebody ought to land on the moon before too long."

He added absorbedly: "Once the Platform is fully equipped, it won't take many rocket pay loads to refill a ship's tanks at the Platform, before it can head on out."

Mathematically, a rocket ship that could leave the Platform with full fuel tanks should have fuel to reach the moon and land on it, and take off again and return to the Platform. The mathematical fact had a peculiar nagging flavor. When a dream is subjected to statistical analysis and the report is in its favor, a dreamer's satisfaction is always diluted by a subconscious feeling that the report is only part of the dream. Everybody worries a little when a cherished dream shows a likelihood of coming true. Some people take firm steps to stop things right there, so a romantic daydream won't be spoiled by transmutation into prosaic fact. But Joe said doggedly: "Twenty ferry trips to pile up fuel, and the twenty-first ship should be able to refuel and go on out. And then somebody will step out on the moon!"

He was disappointed now. He wouldn't be the one to do it. But somebody would.

"You might try for the ferry service," said Sally uneasily.

"I will," said Joe grimly, "but I won't be hoping too much.

125

After all, there are astronomers and physics sharks and such things, who'll be glad to learn to run rockets in order to practice their specialties out of atmosphere."

Sally said mournfully: "I can't seem to say anything to make you feel better!"

"But you do," said Joe. He added grandiloquently, "But for your unflagging faith in me, I would not have the courage to bear the burdens of everyday life."

She stamped her foot.

"Stop it!"

"All right." But he said quietly, "You are a good kid, Sally. You know, it's not too bright of me to mourn."

She drew a deep breath.

"That's better! Now, I want——"

There was a gangling figure walking down the concrete path between the trim, monotonous cottages that were officers' quarters at the Shed.

Joe said sharply: "That's Haney! What's he doing here?" He called, "Haney!"

Haney's manner took on purpose. He came across the grass— the lawns around the officers' quarters contained the only grass in twenty miles.

"Hiya," said Haney uncomfortably. He spoke politely to Sally. "Hiya. Uh—you want to get in on the party, Joe?"

"What kind?"

"The party Mike was talkin' about," said Haney. "He's set it up. He wants me to get you and a kinda—uh—undercover tip-off to Major Holt."

Joe stirred. Sally said hospitably: "Sit down. You've noticed that my father gave you full security clearance, so you can go anywhere?"

Haney perched awkwardly on the edge of the porch.

"Yeah. That's helped with the party. It's how I got here, as far as that goes. Mike's on top of the world."

"Shoot it," said Joe.

"Y'know he's been pretty bitter about things," said Haney carefully. "He's been sayin' that little guys like him ought to be the

126

spacemen. There's half a dozen other little guys been working on the Platform too. They can get in cracks an' buck rivets an' so on. Useful. He's had 'em all hopped up on the fact that the Platform coulda been finished months ago if it'd been built for them, an' they could get to the moon an' back while full-sized guys couldn't an' so on. Remember?"

"I remember," said Sally.

"They've all been beefin' about it," explained Haney. "People know how they feel. So today Mike went and talked to one or two of 'em. An' they started actin' mysterious, passin' messages back an' forth an' so on. Little guys, actin' important. Security guys wouldn't notice 'em much. Y'don't take a guy Mike's size serious, unless you know him. Then he's the same as anybody else. So the security guys didn't pay any attention to him. But some other guys did. Some special other guys. They saw those little fellas actin' like they were cookin' up somethin' fancy. An' they bit."

"Bit?" asked Sally.

"They got curious. So Mike an' his gang got confidential. An' they're going to have help sabotagin' the Platform when the next shift changes. The midgets gettin' even for bein' laughed at, see? They're pretending their plan is that when the Platform's sabotaged—not smashed, but just messed up so it can't take off— the big brass will let 'em take a ferry rocket up in a hurry, an' get it in orbit, an' use it for a Platform until the big Platform can be mended an' sent up. Once they're up there, there's no use tryin' to stop the big Platform. So it can go ahead."

Joe said dubiously: "I think I see...."

"Mike and his gang of little guys are bein' saps—on purpose. If anybody's goin' to pull some fast stuff, next shift change—that's the time everybody's got to! Last chance! Mike and his gang don't know what's gonna happen, but they sure know when! They're invitin' the real saboteurs to make fools of 'em. And what'll happen?"

Joe said drily: "The logical thing would be to feel sorry for the big guys who think they're smarter than Mike."

"Uh-huh," said Haney, deadly serious. "Mike's story is there's half a dozen rocket tubes already loaded. They're goin' to fire those

127

rockets between shifts. The Platform gets shoved off its base an' maybe dented, and so on. Mike's gang say they got the figures to prove they can go up in a ferry rocket an' be a Platform, and the big brass won't have any choice but to let 'em."

Sally said: "I don't think they know how the big brass thinks."

Haney and Joe said together, "No!" and Joe added: "Mike's not crazy! He knows better! But it's a good story for somebody who doesn't know Mike."

Haney said in indignation: "I came out here to ask the Major to help us. The Chief's gettin' a gang together, too. There's some Indians of his tribe that work here. We can count on them for plenty of rough stuff. And there's Joe and me. The point is that Mike's stunt makes it certain that everything busts loose at a time we can know in advance. If the Major gives us a free hand, and then in the last five minutes takes his own measures—so they can't leak out ahead of time and tip off the gangs we want to get—we oughta knock off all the expert saboteurs who know the weak spots in the Platform. For instance those who know that thermite in the gyros would mess everything up all over again."

Joe said quietly: "But Major Holt has to be told well in advance about all this! That's absolute!"

"Yeah," agreed Haney. "But also he has got to keep quiet—not tell anybody else! There've been too many leaks already about too many things. You know that!"

Joe said: "Sally, see if you can get your father to come here and talk. Haney's right. Not in his office. Right here."

Sally got up and went inside the house. She came back with an uneasy expression on her face.

"He's coming. But I couldn't very well tell him what was wanted, and—I'm not sure he's going to be in a mood to listen."

When the Major arrived he was definitely not in a mood to listen. He was a harried man, and he was keyed up to the limit by the multiplied strain due to the imminence of the Platform's take-off. He came back to his house from a grim conference on exactly the subject of how to make preparations against any possible sabotage incidents—and ran into a proposal to stimulate them! He practically exploded. Even if provocation should be given to

128

saboteurs to lure them into showing their hands, this was no time for it! And if it were, it would be security business. It should not be meddled in by amateurs!

Joe said grimly: "I don't mean to be disrespectful, sir, but there's a point you've missed. It isn't thinkable that you'll be able to prevent something from being tried at a time the saboteurs pick. They've got just so much time left, and they'll use it! But Mike's plan would offer them a diversion under cover of which they could pull their own stuff! And besides that, you know your office leaks! You couldn't set up a trick like this through security methods. And for a third fact, this is the one sort of thing no saboteur would expect from your security organization! We caught the saboteurs at the pushpot field by guessing at a new sort of thinking for sabotage. Here's a chance to catch the saboteurs who'll work their heads off in the next twenty-four hours or so, by using a new sort of thinking for security!"

Major Holt was not an easy man to get along with at any time, and this was the worst of all times to differ with him. But he did think straight. He stared furiously at Joe, growing crimson with anger at being argued with. But after he had stared a full minute, the angry flush went slowly away. Then he nodded abruptly.

"There you have a point," he said curtly. "I don't like it. But it is a point. It would be completely the reverse of anything my antagonists could possibly expect. So I accept the suggestion. Now—let us make the arrangements."

He settled down for a quick, comprehensive, detailed plan. In careful consultation with Haney, Joe worked it out. The all-important point was that the Major's part was to be done in completely unorthodox fashion. He would take measures to mesh his actions with those of Mike, the Chief, Haney, and Joe. Each action the Major took and each order he gave he would attend to personally. His actions would be restricted to the last five minutes or less before shift-change time. His orders would be given individually to individuals, and under no circumstances would he transmit any order through anybody else. In every instance, his order would be devised to mean nothing intelligible to its recipient until the time came for obedience.

It was not an easy scheme for the Major to bind himself to. It ran counter to every principle of military thinking save one, which was that it was a good idea to outguess the enemy. At the end he said detachedly: "This is distinctly irregular. It is as irregular as anything could possibly be! But that is why I have agreed to it. It will be at least—unexpected—coming from me!"

Then he smiled without mirth and nodded to Joe and to Haney, and went striding away down the concrete walk to where his car waited.

Haney left a moment later to carry the list of arrangements to the Chief and to Mike. And Joe went into the Shed to do his part.

There was little difference in the appearance of the Shed by night. In the daytime there were long rows of windows in the roof, which let in a vague, dusky, inadequate twilight. At night those windows were shuttered. This meant that the shadows were a little sharper and the contrasts of light and shade a trifle more abrupt. All other changes that Joe could see were the normal ones due to the taking down of scaffolding and the fastening up of rocket tubes. It was clear that the shape of the Platform proper would be obscure when all its rocket tubes were fast in place.

Joe went to look at the last pushpots, and they were ready to be taken over to their own field for their flight test before use. There were extras, anyhow, beyond the number needed to lift the Platform. He found himself considering the obvious fact that after the Platform was aloft, they would be used to launch the ferry rockets, too.

Then he moved toward the center of the Shed. A whole level of scaffolding came apart and its separate elements were bundled together as he watched. Slings lowered the bundles down to waiting trucks which would carry them elsewhere. There were mixing trucks still pouring out their white paste for the lining of the rocket tubes, and their product went up and vanished into the gaping mouths of the giant wire-wound pipes.

Presently Joe went into the maze of piers under the Space Platform itself. He came to the temporary stairs he had reason to remember. He nodded to the two guards there.

"I want to take another look at that gadget we installed," he said.

One of the guards said good-naturedly: "Major Holt said to pass you any time."

He ascended and went along the curious corridor—it had handgrips on the walls so a man could pull himself along it when there was no weight—and went to the engine room. He heard voices. They were speaking a completely unintelligible language. He tensed.

Then the Chief grinned at him amiably. He was in the engine room and with him were no fewer than eight men of his own coppery complexion.

"Here's some friends of mine," he explained, and Joe shook hands with black-haired, dark-skinned men who were named Charley Spotted Dog and Sam Fatbelly and Luther Red Cow and other exotic things. The Chief said exuberantly, "Major Holt told the guards to let me pass in some Indian friends, so I took my gang on a guided tour of the Platform. None of 'em had ever been inside before. And——"

"I heard you talking Indian," said Joe.

"You're gonna hear some more," said the Chief. "We're the first war party of my tribe in longer'n my grandpa woulda thought respectable!"

Joe found it difficult to restrain a smile. The Chief took him off to one side.

"Fella," he said kindly, "it bothers you, this business, because it ain't organized. That's what this world needs, Joe. Everything figured out by slide rules an' such—it's civilized, but it ain't human! What everybody oughta be is a connoisseur of chaos, like me. Quit worryin' an' get outside and pick up that security guy the Major was gonna send to meet you!"

He gave Joe an amiable shove and rejoined his fellow Mohawks, each of whom, Joe noticed suddenly, had somewhere on his person a twelve-inch Stillson wrench or a reasonable facsimile to serve as a substitute tomahawk. They grinned at him as he departed.

131

At the bottom of the flight of narrow wooden steps there was a third security man. He greeted Joe.

"Major Holt told me to pick you up," he observed.

Joe walked to one side with him. Major Holt had promised to send a first-class man to meet Joe at this place, with orders to take instructions from Joe. Joe said curtly: "You're to snag as many Security men as you can, place them more or less out of sight under the Platform here, and tell them to turn off their walkie-talkies and wait. No matter what happens, they're to wait right here until they're needed, right here!"

He looked harassedly around him. The Security man nodded and moved casually away. This was close timing. Something made Joe look up. He saw the catwalk gallery nearly overhead. The expected guard was there. Haney, though, was with him. There was nothing else in sight. Not yet. But Haney was on the job. Joe saw a Security man step out of sight in the scaffolding. He saw his own assigned security man speak to another, who wandered casually toward the Platform's base.

Minutes passed. Only Joe could have noticed, because he was watching for it. There were eight or nine Security men posted within call. They had their walkie-talkies turned off and would be subject only to his orders if an emergency arose.

Gongs began to ring all around the edge of the Shed. They set up a horrendous clanging. This was not an alarm, but simply the notice of change-of-shift time.

There was a marked change in the noises overhead. A crane pulled back. Hammerings dwindled and stopped. There were the sounds of pipes, combined to form the scaffolds, being taken apart for removal. A sling-load of pipe touched the floor and stayed there. The crane's internal-combustion motor stopped. Its operator stepped down to the floor and headed for the exit. Hoists descended and men moved across the floor. Other men scrambled down ladders. The floor became dotted with figures moving toward the doors through which men went out to get on the busses for Bootstrap.

Nothing happened. More long minutes passed. The shift brought out by the busses was going through the check-over process in the incoming screen room. Joe knew that Major Holt had, within the past five minutes, gathered together a tight-knit bunch of armed security men to be available for anything that might turn up. The men doing the normal shift-change screening were shorthanded in consequence.

The floor next to the exits became crowded, but the central area of the floor was cleared. One truck was stalled at the swing-up truck doors. Its driver ground the starter insistently.

Suddenly there was a high-pitched yell away up on the Platform. Then there was a shot. Its echoes rang horribly in the resonant interior of the Shed. Joe's own special security man hurried to him, his face tense.

"What about that?"

"Hold everything," said Joe grimly. "That's taken care of."

It was. That was Mike's gang—miniature humans popping out of hiding to offer battle with missiles carefully prepared beforehand against their alleged associates in sabotage. One of the associates had drawn a gun and fired. But Mike's gang had help. Out of small air locks devised to make the Platform's skin accessible to its crew on every side—provided they wore space suits—dark-skinned men appeared.

The security man's walkie-talkie under his shoulder made a buzzing sound. He reached for it.

"Forget it!" snapped Joe. "That's not for you! You've got your orders! Stay here!"

There was a sudden growling uproar where men were crowding to get out of the Shed. Thick, billowing smoke appeared. There was a crashing explosion. The men eddied and milled crazily.

The motor of the stalled truck caught. It moved toward the door, which opened, swinging up and high. Two trucks came roaring in. They raced for the Platform. And as they raced inside, their camouflaged loads clattered off and men showed instead. The guards by the doorway began to shoot.

"That's what we've got to stop!" snapped Joe.

He began to run, his pistol out. There was suddenly a small army—gathered by his orders—which materialized in the dim

133

space under the Platform. It raced to guard against this evidently well-planned invasion.

The harsh, tearing rattle of a machine gun sounded from somewhere high up. Joe knew what it was. Mike's whole scheme had been intended to force all sabotage efforts to take place at a single instant. Part of the preparation was authority for Haney to drag in two machine guns from an outer watching-post and mount them to cover the interior of the Shed when the general attack began.

Those machine guns were shooting at the trucks. Splinters sprang up from the wood-block floor. Then, abruptly, one of the trucks vanished in a monstrous, actinic flash of blue-white flame and a roar so horrible that it was not sound but pure concussion. The other truck keeled over and crashed from the blast, but did not explode. Men jumped from it. There must have been screamed orders, but Joe could hear nothing at all. He only saw men waving their arms, and others seized things from the toppled load and rushed toward him, and he began to shoot as he ran to meet them.

Now, belatedly, the sirens of the Shed screamed their alarm, and choppy yappings set up as the siren wails rose in pitch. Over by the exit pistols cracked. Something fell with a ghastly crash not ten feet from where Joe ran. It was a man's body, toppled from somewhere high up on the structure that was the most important man-made thing in all the world. A barbaric war whoop sounded among the echoes of other tumult.

A Security man shot, and one of the running figures toppled and slid, his burden—which must certainly be a bomb—rolling ridiculously. There had been two trucks that plunged through the swing-up door. They had raced for the spaces under the Platform at the exact time when the floor would be clear, because all work had stopped. Under the Platform, the trucks were to have been detonated. At the very least, they would have rent and torn it horribly. They might have broken its back. And surely one truck should have made it. But there should not have been machine guns ready trained to shoot. Now the load of desperate men from the overturned survivor scurried for the Platform with parts of its cargo. If they could fight their way inside the Platform, they could blast its hull open, or demolish its controls or shatter its air pumps and its gyros and turn its air tanks into sieves. Anything that could be damaged would delay the take-off and so expose the Platform to further and perhaps more successful attack.

There were more pistol shots. A group of men fought their way out of the incoming screening rooms and raced for the center of the Shed. (Later, it would be found they had slabs of explosive inside their garments, and detonation caps to set them off.) Somewhere another door opened, and Security men came out with flickering pistols, Major Holt leading them. He had started out to fight off the truck-borne attack, but he was bound to be too late. Joe's followers were trying to take care of that. The scuttling men from the incoming rooms were Major Holt's first prey. They were shot as they ran.

Joe stumbled and fell and he heard guns crackling. As he scrambled up he pitched into a running figure that snarled as Joe hit him. And then he was fighting for his life.

This was under the Platform and in the middle of confusion many times confounded. Joe caught a wrist that held a gun. He knew his assailant had a bomb slung over one shoulder and right now had one hand free for combat. Joe instinctively tried to batter his enemy with his own pistol, instead of pushing the muzzle against the man's body and pulling the trigger. He struck a flailing blow, and his hand and the weapon struck a metal brace. The blow cut his knuckles and paralyzed his fingers. Despairingly he felt the pistol slipping from his grasp. Then his assailant brought up his knee viciously, but it hit Joe's thigh instead of his groin, and Joe flung his weight furiously forward and they toppled to the ground together.

There was fighting all around him. The machine guns rasped again—there was a burst of tracer-bullet fire. The panicked men by the exit tried to surge out through the swinging doors. But the tracers marked a line they must not cross. They checked. Once a gun flashed so close by Joe's eyes that it blinded him. And once somebody fell over both himself and his antagonist, who writhed like an eel possessed of desperate strength past belief.

Joe could really know only his private part in the struggle

135

down in the murky tangle of the scaffold base. But there was fighting up on the Platform itself. A savagely grinning Mohawk wrestled furiously with a man on one of the rocket tubes. An incendiary device in the saboteur's pocket ignited, and it flamed red-hot and he screamed as it burned its way out of his garments. The Mohawk flung the man fiercely clear, to crash horribly on the far-distant floor, and then kicked the incendiary off. It fell after the man and hit and burst, and it was thermite which surrounded itself with a column of acrid smoke from seared wood blocks.

There was fighting by the exit doors. There was an ululating uproar in the incoming screening room, and a war whoop from the top of the Platform. A saboteur tried to crawl into an air-lock entrance, and he got his head and shoulders in, but a copper-skinned Indian held his forehead still and chopped down with the side of his hand on that man's neck. Underneath the Platform was panting chaos, with pistol shots and hand-to-hand struggles everywhere. The force Joe had gathered fought valiantly, but four invaders got to the foot of the wooden steps, where there were two guards. Then there were only two saboteurs left to scramble desperately up the steps over the dead guards' bodies and head toward the Platform door, but the Chief appeared swinging a twelve-inch Stillson. He let it go, precisely like a skillfully flung tomahawk, and leaped down sixteen steps squarely onto the body of the other man. A gun flashed, but then there was only squirming struggle on the floor.

Mike the midget, inside the Platform, found one bloodied, panting, sobbing man who somehow had gotten inside. And Mike brought down a spanner from a ladder step, and swarmed upon his half-conscious victim, and hit him again, and then stayed on guard until somebody arrived who was big enough to carry the saboteur away.

And all this while, Joe struggled with only one man. It was a horrible struggle, because the man had a bomb and he might manage to set it off or it might go off of itself. It was a ghastly struggle, because the man had the strength and desperation of a maniac—and practiced the tactics. Joe pounded the hand that held the gun upon the floor, and it hit something and exploded smokily and fell clear. But that made things worse. While struggling to kill Joe with the revolver, his antagonist had had only five fingers with which to gouge out Joe's eyes or tear away his ears or rend his flesh. But with no pistol he had ten, and he fought like a wild beast. He even breathed like an animal. He began to pant—thick, guttural pantings that had the quality of hellish hate. And then there was a surging of bodies—Major Holt's reserve was arriving very late in the center of the Shed—and then a struggling group trampled all over the pair who squirmed and fought on the ground, and a heavy boot jammed down Joe's head and he felt teeth sink in his throat. They dug into his flesh, worrying and tearing....

Joe used his knee in a frenzy of revulsion—used his knee as the other man had tried to use his in the first instant of battle. The man beneath him screamed as an animal would scream, and Joe jerked his bleeding throat free. In hysterical horror he pounded his antagonist's head on the floor until the man went limp....

And then he heard a grim voice saying: "Quit it or you get your head blown off! Quit it——" And Joe panted: "It's about time you guys got here! This man came in on that truck. Watch out for that bomb he's got slung on him...."

CHAPTER 12

The incoming shift had a messy clean-up job to do. It was accomplished only because security men abruptly took over the work of gang bosses, and all ordinary labor on the Platform was put aside until normal operations were again possible. Even that would not have been feasible but for the walkie-talkies the security men wore. As the situation was sorted out, it was explained to them, and they relayed the news for the satisfaction of the curiosity of those who worked under them. No work—no explanation. It produced immediate and satisfactory co-operation all around.

There had been four separate and independent attempts to wreck the Platform at the same time. One was, of course, the plan of those sympathetic characters who had volunteered to help Mike and his gang win the status of spacemen by firing the Platform's rockets. There were not many of them, and they had lost heavily. They'd had thermite bombs to destroy the Platform's vitals. Ultimately the survivors talked freely, if morosely, and that was that.

There had been a particularly ungifted attempt to cause panic in the incoming shift in the rooms where its members were screened before admission to work. Somebody had tried to establish complete confusion there by firing revolver shots in the crowd, expecting the workers to break through to the floor and assigned gentlemen with slabs of explosive to get to the Platform with them. The gentlemen with the explosives had run into Major Holt's security reserve, and they got nowhere. The creators of panic with revolver shots were finally rescued from their shift-mates and more or less scraped up from the screening-room floor—they were in very bad shape—and carted off to be patched up for questioning. The members of this group had been impractical idealists, and besides, some of them had lost their nerve, as was evidenced by the discovery of abandoned explosives and detonators in the locker room and men's room of the Shed.

The most dangerous attempt was, of course, that perfectly planned and co-ordinated assault which had been merely carried out at its original time, without either being hastened or delayed by Mike's activities. That plan had been beautifully contrived, and it would certainly have been successful but for the machine-gun bullets from the gallery and the fight Joe's followers put up underneath the Platform.

The exact instant when the whole Shed would be most nearly empty had been fixed upon, and three separate units had worked in perfect timing. There'd been the man in the stalled truck. He'd delayed his exit from the Shed to the precise fraction of a second to get the doors open at the perfect instant. The explosive-laden trucks had raced in at the exact second when they were most certain to get underneath the Platform and detonate their cargoes. There'd been a perfect diversion planned for that, too. Smoke bombs and explosions in the outgoing screening rooms had created real panic, and but for Joe's order for his group's walkie-talkies to be turned off would have drawn every security man on duty to that spot.

Mike's trick, then, had brought some saboteurs into the open, but had merely happened to coincide with the most dangerous and well-organized coup of all. However, it was due to his trick that the Platform was not now a wreck.

There was also another break that was sheer coincidence. It was a discovery that could not possibly have turned up save in a situation of pure chaos artificially induced. Joe had had to react in a personal and vengeful way to the manner in which his especial antagonist had fought him. One expects a man to fight fair by instinct, and to turn to fouls—if he does—in desperation only. But Joe's personal opponent hadn't tried a single fair trick. It was as if he'd never heard of a fist blow, but only of murder and mayhem. Joe felt an individual enmity toward him.

Joe didn't consider himself the most urgent of the injured, when doctors and nurses took up the work of patching, but Sally was there to help, and she went deathly pale when she saw his bloodstained throat. She dragged him quickly to a doctor. And the doctor looked at Joe and dropped everything else.

But it wasn't too serious. The antiseptics hurt, and the stitching was unpleasant, but Joe was more worried by the knowledge that Sally was standing there and suffering for him. When he got up from the emergency operating table, the doctor nodded grimly to him.

"That was close!" said the doctor. "Whoever chewed you was working for your jugular vein, and he was halfway through the wall when he stopped. A fraction of an inch more, and he'd have had you!"

"Thanks," said Joe. His neck felt clumsy with bandages, and when he tried to turn his head the stitches hurt.

Sally's hand trembled in his when she led him away.

"I didn't think I'd ever dislike anybody so much," said Joe angrily, "as I did that man while he was chewing my throat. We were trying to kill each other, of course, but—confound it, people don't bite!"

"Did you—kill him?" asked Sally in a shaky voice. "Not that I'll mind! I would have hated the thought ordinarily, but——"

Joe halted. There was a row of stretchers—not too long, at that—in the emergency-hospital space. He looked down at the unconscious man who'd fought him.

"There he is!" he said irritably. "I banged him pretty hard. I don't like to hate anybody, but the way he fought——"

Sally's teeth chattered suddenly. She called to one of the security men standing guard by the stretchers.

"I—think my—father is going to want to talk to him," she said unsteadily. "Don't—let him be taken away to the hospital until Dad knows, please."

She started away, her face dead-white and her hand stone-cold.

"What's the matter?" demanded Joe.

"S-sabotage," said Sally in an indescribable tone that had a suggestion of heartbreak.

She went into her father's office alone. She came out again with him, and her father looked completely stricken. Miss Ross, his secretary, was with him, too. Her face was like a mask of marble. She had always been a plain woman, a gloomy one, a morbid one. But at the new and horrible look on her face Joe turned his eyes away.

Then Sally was crying beside him, and he put his arm clumsily around her and let her sob on his shoulder, completely puzzled.

He didn't find out until later what the trouble was. The man who'd tried so earnestly to kill him was Miss Ross's fiancé. She had met this man during a vacation, as a government secretary, and he was a refugee with an exotic charm that would have fascinated a much more personable and beautiful woman than Miss Ross. They had a whirlwind romance. He confided to her his terror of emissaries from his native country who might kill him. And of course she was more fascinated still. When he asked her to marry him she accepted his proposal. Then, just two weeks before her assignment to the Space Platform project, he vanished. Miss Ross was desperate and lovesick.

One day her telephone rang and his anguished voice told her he'd been abducted, and if she told the police he would be tortured to death. He begged her not to do anything to cause him more torment than was already his.

She'd been trying to keep him alive ever since. Once, when she couldn't bring herself to carry out an order she'd been given—with threats of torment to him if she failed—she'd received a human finger in the mail, and a scrawled and blood-stained note which cried out of unspeakable torment and begged her not to doom him to more.

So Miss Ross, who was Major Holt's secretary and one of his most trusted assistants, had been giving information to one group of saboteurs all the while. She was the most dangerous security leak in the whole Platform project.

But her fiancé wasn't a captive. He was the head of that group of saboteurs. He'd made love to her and proposed to her merely to prepare her to supply the information he wanted. He needed only to write a sufficiently agonized note, or gasp tormented pleas on a telephone, to get what he wanted.

Incidentally, he still had all his fingers when Joe knocked him cold.

Sally had recognized him as the subject of a snapshot she'd once seen Miss Ross crying over. Miss Ross had hidden it hastily and told her it was someone she had once loved, now dead. And this inadvertent disclosure that Miss Ross was the security leak the Major had never had a clue to could only have come about through such confusion as Mike had instigated and Haney and the Chief and Joe had organized. But Joe learned those facts only later.

At the moment, there was still the Platform to be gotten aloft. And there was plenty of work to do. There were two small rips in the plating, caused by fragments of the exploded truck. There were some bullet holes. The Platform could resist small meteorites at forty-five miles a second, but a high-velocity small-arm projectile could puncture it. Those scars of battle had to be welded shut. The rest of the scaffolding had to come down and the rest of the rocket tubes had to be affixed. And there was cleaning up to be done.

These things occupied the shift that came on at the time of the multiple sabotage assaults. At first the work was ragged. But the policy of turning the Security men into news broadcasters worked well. After all, the Platform was a construction job and the men who worked on it were not softies. Most of them had seen men killed before. Before the shift was half over, a definite work rhythm was evident. Men had begun to take an even greater pride in the thing they had built, because it had been assailed and not destroyed. And the job was almost over.

Sally went back to her father's quarters, to try to sleep. Joe stayed in the Shed. His throat was painful enough so that he didn't want to go to bed until he was genuinely tired, and he was thoroughly wrought up.

Mike the midget had gone peacefully to sleep again, curled up in a corner of the outgoing screening room. His fellow midgets talked satisfiedly among themselves. Presently, to show their superiority to mere pitched battles, two of them brought out a miniature pack of cards and started a card game while they waited for a bus to take them back to Bootstrap.

The Chief's Indian associates loafed comfortably while waiting for the same busses. Later they would put in for overtime—and get it. Haney mourned that he had been remote from the scene of action, and was merely responsible for the presence and placing and firing of the machine guns that had certainly kept the Platform from being blown up from below.

It seemed that nothing else would happen to bother anybody. But there was one thing more.

That thing happened just two hours before it was time for the shift to change once again, and when normal work was back in progress in the Shed. Everything seemed fully organized and serene. Everything in the Shed had settled down, and nothing had happened outside.

There was ample exterior protection, of course, but the outside-guard system hadn't had anything to do for a very long time. Men at radar screens were bored and sleepy from sheer inactivity and silence. Pilots in jet planes two miles and five miles and eight miles high had long since grown weary of the splendid view below them. After all, one can get very used to late, slanting moonlight on cloud masses far underneath, and bright and hostile-seeming stars overhead.

So the thing was well timed.

A Canadian station noticed the pip on its radar screen first. The radar observer was puzzled by it. It could have been a meteor, and the Canadian observer at first thought it was. But it wasn't going quite fast enough, and it lasted too long. It was traveling six hundred seventy-two miles an hour, and it was headed due south at sixty thousand feet. The speed could have been within reason—provided it didn't stay constant. But it did. There was something traveling south at eleven miles a minute or better. A mile in five-plus seconds. It didn't slow. It didn't drop.

The Canadian radarman debated painfully. He stopped his companion from the reading of a magazine article about chinchilla breeding in the home. He showed him the pip, still headed south and almost at the limit of this radar instrument's range. They discussed the thing dubiously. They decided to report it.

They had a little trouble getting the call through. The night long-distance operators were sleepy. Because of the difficulty of making the call, the radarmen became obstinate and insisted on putting it through. They reported to Ottawa that some object flying at sixty thousand feet and six hundred seventy-two miles an hour was crossing Canada headed for the United States.

There was a further time loss. Somebody in authority had to be awakened, and somebody had to decide that a further report was justified. Then the trick had to be accomplished, and a sleepy man

143

in a bathrobe and slippers listened and said sleepily, "Oh, of course you'll tell the Americans. It's only neighborly!" and padded back to his bed to go to sleep again. Then he waked up suddenly and began to sweat. He'd realized that this might be the beginning of atomic war. So he set phone bells to jangling furiously all over Canada, and jet planes began to boom in the darkness.

But there was only one object in the sky. Over the Dakotas it went higher. It went to seventy thousand feet, and then eighty. How this was managed is not completely known, because there are still some details of that flight that have never been completely explained. But certainly jatos flared briefly at some point, and the object reached ninety thousand feet where a jet motor would certainly be useless. And then, almost certainly, rockets flared once more and well south of the Dakotas it started down in a trajectory like that of an artillery shell, but with considerably higher speed than most artillery shells achieve.

It was at about this time that the siren in the Shed began its choppy, hiccoughing series of warm-up notes. The news from Canada arrived, as a matter of fact, some thirty seconds after the outer-perimeter radar screen around the Platform gave its warning. Then there was no hesitation or delay at all. Men were already tumbling out of bed at three airfields, buckling helmets and hoping their oxygen tanks would function properly. Then the radars atop the Shed itself picked up the moving speck. And small blue-white flames began to rise from the ground and go streaking away in the darkness in astonishing numbers.

The covers of the guns at the top of the Shed slid aside. Miles away, jet planes shot skyward, and newly wakened pilots looked at their night-fighting instruments and swore unbelievingly at the speed they were told the plunging object was making. The jet pilots gave their motors everything they could take, but it didn't look good.

The planes of the jet umbrella over the Shed stopped cruising and sprinted. And they were the only ones likely to get in front of the object in time.

Inside the Shed, the siren howled dismally and all the Security men were snapping: "Radar alarm! All out! Radar alarm! All out!"

And men were moving fast, too. Some came down from the Platform on hoists, dropping with reckless speed to the floor level. Some didn't wait for a turn at that. They slid down one upright, swung around the crosspiece on the level below, and slid down another vertical pipe. For a minute or more it looked as if the scaffolds oozed black droplets which slid down its pipes. But the drops were men. The floor became speckled and spotted with dots running for its exits.

The siren ceased its wailing and its noise went down and down in pitch until it was a baritone moan that dropped to bass and ceased. Then there was no sound but the men moving to get out of the Shed. There were trucks, too. Those that had been loading with dismantled scaffolding roared for the doors to get out and away. Some men jumped on board as they passed. The exit doors swung up to let them go.

But it was very quiet in the Shed, at that. There was no noise but a few fleeing trucks, and the murmur which was the voices of the Security men hurrying the work crew out. There was less to hear than went on ordinarily. And it was a long distance across the floor of the Shed.

Joe stood with his fists clenched absurdly. This could only be an air attack. An air attack could only mean an atom-bomb attack. And if there was an atom bomb dropped on the Shed, there'd be no use getting outside. It wouldn't be merely a fission bomb. It would be a hell bomb—a bomb which used the kind of bomb that shattered Hiroshima only as a primer for the real explosive. Nobody could hope to get beyond the radius of its destruction before it hit!

Joe heard himself raging. He'd thought of Sally. She'd be in the range of annihilation, too. And Joe knew such fury and hatred— because of Sally—that he forgot everything else.

He didn't run. He couldn't escape. He couldn't fight back. But because he hated, he had to do something to defy.

He found himself moving toward the Platform, his jaws clenched. It was pure, blind, instinctive defiance.

He was not the only one to have that reaction. Men running toward the sidewall exits began to get out of breath from their

145

running. They slowed. Presently they stopped. They scowled and raged, like Joe. Some of them looked with burning eyes up at the roof of the Shed, though their thoughts went on beyond it. The security guards repeated, "Radar alarm! All out! Radar alarm! All out!"

Someone snarled, "Nuts to that!"

Joe saw a man walking in the same direction as himself. He was walking deliberately back to the Platform. Somebody else was headed back too....

Very peculiarly, almost all the men on the floor had ceased to run. They began to gather in little groups. They knew flight was useless. They talked briefly. Profanely. Here and there men started disgustedly back toward the Platform. Their lips moved in expressions of furious scorn. Their scorn was of themselves.

There was a gathering of men about the base of the framework that still partly veiled the Platform. They tended to face outward, angrily, and to clench their fists.

Then somebody started an engine. A man began to climb furiously back to where he had been at work. Quite unreasonably, other men followed him.

Hammers began defiantly and enragedly to sound.

The work crew in the Shed went defiantly and furiously back to work. A clamor was set up that was almost the normal working noise. It was the only possible way in which those men could express the raging contempt they felt for those who would destroy the thing they worked on.

But there were some other men who could do more. There were three levels of jet planes above the Shed, and they could dive. The highest one got first to the line along which the missile from an unknown place was plunging toward the Shed. That plane steadied on a collision course and let go its wing load of rockets. It peeled off and got out of the way. Seconds later the others from the jet umbrella were arriving. A tiny spray of proximity-fused rockets blazed furiously toward the invisible thing from the heights.

Other planes and yet others came hurtling to the line their radars briskly computed for them. There were more rockets....

The black-painted thing with more than the speed of an

artillery shell plunged into a miniature hail of rockets. They flamed viciously. Half a dozen—a dozen—explosions that were pure futility.

Then there was an explosion that was not. Nobody saw it, because its puny detonation was instantly wiped out in a blaze of such incredible incandescence that the aluminum paint on jet planes still miles away was scorched and blistered instantly. The light of that flare was seen for hundreds of miles. The sound—later on—was heard farther still. And the desert vegetation miles below the hell bomb showed signs of searing when the morning came.

But the thing from the north was vaporized, utterly, some forty-five miles from its target. The damage it did was negligible.

The work on the preparation for the Platform's take-off went on. When the all-clear signal sounded inside the Shed, nobody paid any attention. They were too busy.

CHAPTER 13

On the day of the take-off there were a number of curious side-effects from the completion of the Space Platform. There was a very small country on the other side of the world which determined desperately to risk its existence on the success of the Platform's flight. It had to choose between abject submission to a powerful neighbor, or the possibility of a revolution in which its neighbor's troops would take on the semblance of citizens for street-fighting purposes. If the Platform got aloft, it could defy its neighbor. And in a grim gamble, it did.

There was also a last-ditch fight in the United Nations, wherein the Platform was denounced and a certain block of associated countries issued an ultimatum, threatening to bolt the international organization if the Platform went aloft. And again there had to be a grim gamble. If the Platform did not take to space and so furnish ultimately a guarantee of peace, the United Nations would face the alternatives of becoming a military alliance for atomic war, or something less than an international debating society.

Of course there were less significant results. There were already fourteen popular songs ready for broadcast, orchestrated and rehearsed with singers ready to saturate the ears of the listening public. They ranged from We've Got a Warship in the Sky, which was more or less jingoistic, to a boy-and-girl melody entitled We'll Have a Moon Just for Us Two. The latter tune had been stolen from a hit of four years before, which in turn had been stolen from a hit of six years before that, and it had been stolen from a still earlier bit of Bach, so it was a rather pretty melody.

And of course there was a super-colossal motion picture epic in color and with musical numbers, champing in its film cans for simultaneous first-run showings in eight different key cities. It was titled To the Stars, and three separate endings had been filmed, of which the appropriate one would of course be used in the eight separate world premières. One ending had the Platform fail due to sabotage, and the hero—played by an actor who had interrupted his seventh honeymoon to play the part—splendidly prepared to build it all over again. The second ending closed with the Platform headed for Alpha Centaurus—which was hardly the intention of anybody outside of filmdom. The third ending was secret, but it was said that hard-boiled motion-picture executives had cried like babies when it was thrown on preview screens.

These, of course, were merely sidelights. They were not very important in the Shed. There, work went on at a feverish rate although there was no longer any construction work to be done. In theory, therefore, the members of welders and pipe-fitters and steel-construction and electrical and other unions should have retired gracefully to Bootstrap. Members of building-maintenance and rigging and wrecking and other assorted unions should have been gathered together in far cities, screened by security, and brought to Bootstrap and paid overtime to pull up wood-block flooring and unbolt and jack out the proper sections of the Shed's eastern wall.

But if there had been anything of that sort tried, it would have produced bloodshed. The men who'd built the Platform were going to see it depart this Earth or else. They'd never have a second chance. It would work the first time or it wouldn't work at all.

So the Platform was made ready for its take-off by the men who had made it. A gigantic section—two full gores—of the Shed's wall was unbolted in two pieces, and each piece thrust outward at the top and bottom, so that they were offset from the rest of the huge half-globe. There were hundreds of wheels at their bottom which for the first time touched the sixteen lines of rails laid with unbelievable solidity around the outside of the Shed. And then the monstrous sections were rolled aside. A vast opening resulted, and morning sunlight smote for the first time mankind's very first space craft.

Joe saw the sunlight strike, and his first sensation was of disappointment. The normal shape of the Platform was ungainly, but now it was practically hidden by the solid-fuel rockets which would consume themselves in their firing. Also, the floor of the Shed looked strange. It was littered with the clumsy shapes of pushpots, trucked to this place in an unending stream all night long. A very young lieutenant from the pushpot airfield hunted up

149

Joe and assured him that every drop of fuel in every pushpot's tanks had been tested twice—once in the storage tanks, and again in the pushpots. Joe thanked him very politely.

There was no longer any scaffolding. There were no trucks left except two gigantic cranes, which could handle the pushpots like so many toys. And the effect of sunlight pouring into the Shed seemed strange indeed.

Outside, there were carpenters hammering professionally upon a hasty grandstand of timber. Most of the carpenters would have been handier with rivet guns or welding torches, but it would have been indiscreet to comment. As fast as a final timber was spiked in place, somebody hastily wound it with very tawdry bunting. Men were stringing wires to the grandstand, and other men were setting up television and movie cameras. Two Security men grimly stood by each camera amid a glittering miscellany of microphones.

Joe was lucky. Or perhaps Sally pulled wires. Anyhow, the two of them had a vantage point for which many other people would have paid astonishing sums. They waited where the circular ramp between the two skins of the Shed was broken by the removal of the doorway. They were halfway up the curve of the Shed's roof, at the edge of the great opening, and they could see everything, from the pushpot pilots as they were checked into their contraptions, to the sedate arrival of the big brass at the grandstand below.

There was a reverberant humming from the Shed now. It might have been the humming of wind blowing across its open section. Joe and Sally saw a grim knot of Security men escorting four crew members to a flight of wooden steps that led up to a lower air-lock door—Joe had reason to remember that door—and watched them enter and close the air lock behind them. Then the security men pulled away the wooden stairs and hauled them completely away. There were a very few highly trusted men making final inspections of the Platform's exterior. One of them was nearly on a level with Joe and Sally. Other men were already lowering themselves down on ropes that they later jerked free, but this last man on top did a very human thing. When he'd finished his check-up to the last least detail, he pulled something out of his hip pocket. It was a tobacco can full of black paint. There was a brush with it. He painted his name on the silvery plates of the Platform, "C. J. Adams, Jr.," and satisfiedly began his descent to the ground. His name would go up with the Platform and be visible for uncounted generations—if all went well. He reached the ground and walked away, contented.

The cranes began their task. Each one reached down deliberately and picked up a pushpot. They swung the pushpots to vertical positions and presented them precisely to the Platform's side. They clung there ridiculously. Magnetic grapples, of course. Joe and Sally, at the end of the corridor in the wall, could see the heads of the pushpot pilots in their plastic domes.

Music blared from behind the grandstand. The seats were being filled. But naturally, the least important personages were arriving first. There were women in costumes to which they had given infinite thought—and nobody looked at them except other women. There was khaki. There were gray business suits—slide-rule men, these, who had done the brain-work behind the Platform's design. Then black broadcloth. Politicians, past question. There is nothing less impressive from a height of two hundred feet than a pot-bellied man in black broadcloth walking on the ground.

There were men in uniforms which were not of the United States armed forces. They ran heavily to medals, which glittered. There were more arrivals, and more, and more. The newsreel and TV cameras nosed around.

The cranes worked methodically. They dipped, and deftly picked up a thing shaped like the top half of a loaf of bread. They swung that metal thing to the Platform's side. Each time it clung fast, like a snail or slug to the surface on which it crawls. Many pushpots clung even to the rocket tubes—the same tubes that would presently burn away and vanish. So Joe and Sally saw the pushpots in a new aspect: blunt metal slugs with gaping mouths which were their air scoops.

The tinny music from below cut off. Somebody began an oration. The men who had built the Platform were not interested in fine phrases, but this event was broadcast everywhere, and some people might possibly tune to the channels that carried the speakers and their orations rather than the channels that showed the huge, bleak, obscured shape of the monster that was headed either for empty space or pure disaster.

The speaker stopped, and another took his place. Then another. One man spoke for less than a minute, and the stands went wild! But the one who followed made splendid gestures. He talked and talked and talked. The cranes cleaned up the last of the waiting pushpots, and the Platform itself was practically invisible.

The cranes backed off and went away, clanking. The orator raised his voice. It made small echoes in the vast cavern that was the Shed. Somebody plucked the speaker's arm. He ended abruptly and sat down, wiping his forehead with a huge blue handkerchief.

There was a roar. A pushpot had started its motor. Another roar. Another. One by one, the multitude of clustering objects added to the din. In the open a single jet was appalling. Here, the noise became a sound which was no longer a sound. It became a tumult which by pure volume ceased to be anything one's ears could understand. It reached a peak and held there. Then, abruptly, all the motors slackened in unison, and then roared more loudly. The group controls within the Platform were being tested. Three— four—five times the tumult faded to the merely unbearable and went up to full volume again.

Joe felt Sally plucking at his arm. He turned, and saw a jet plane's underbelly, very close, and its swept-back wings. It was climbing straight up. Then he saw another jet plane streaking for the great dome's open door. It moved with incredible velocity. It jerked upward and climbed over the Shed's curve and was gone. But there were others and others and others.

These were the fighter ships of the jet-plane guard. For months on end they had flown above the Shed, protecting it. Now they were going aloft to relieve the present watchers. They were rising to spread out as an interceptor screen for hundreds of miles in every direction, in case somebody should be so foolish as to try again the exploit of the night before. They would not see the monster in the Shed again. So in a single line which reached to the horizon, they made this roaring run for the one last glimpse which was their right. Joe saw tiny specks come streaking down out of the sky to queue up for this privileged view of the Platform before it rose.

Suddenly they were gone, and Joe felt that tingling sense of pride which never comes from the sensation of sharing in mere power or splendor or pompous might, but is so certain when the human touch modifies magnificence.

And then the roaring of the pushpot engines achieved an utterly impossible volume. The whole interior of the Shed was misty now, but shining in the morning light.

And the Platform moved.

At first it was a mere stirring. It turned ever so slightly to one side, pivoting on the ways that had supported it during building. It turned back and to the other side. The vapor thickened. From each jet motor a blast of blue-white flame poured down, and the moisture in the earth was turning into steam and stray wood-blocks into acrid smoke. The Platform turned precisely and exactly back to its original position, and Joe's heart pounded in his throat, because he knew that the turning had been done with the gyros, and they had been handled by the pilot gyros for which he was responsible.

Then the Platform moved again. It lifted by inches and swayed forward. It checked, and lurched again, and went staggering toward the great opening before it. A part of its base gouged a deep furrow in the earthen floor.

The noise increased from the incredible to the inconceivable. It seemed as if all the thunders since time began had returned to bellow because the Platform moved.

And it floated and bumped out of the Shed. It staggered toward the east. Its keel was perhaps, at this point, as much as three feet above the ground, but the jet motors cast up blinding clouds of dust and smoke and even those afoot could not be sure.

There was confusion. The smoke and vapor splashed out in every possible direction. Joe saw frantic movement, and he realized that the uniforms and the frock coats were scrambling to escape the fumes. The khaki-tinted specks which were men seemed to run. The frock coats ran. The carefully-thought-out brighter specks which were women ran gasping and choking from the smoke. One stout figure toppled, scrambled up, and scuttled frantically for safety.

But the Platform was in motion now. It was a hundred yards beyond the Shed wall. Two hundred. Three.... It slowly gathered

153

speed. A half-mile from the Shed it was definitely clear of the ground. It left a trail of scorched, burnt desert behind....

It moved almost swiftly, now. Two miles from the Shed it was fifteen feet above the earth. Three miles, and a clear strip of sunlight showed beneath it. And it was still accelerating. At four miles and five and six....

It was aloft, climbing with seemingly infinite slowness, with all the hundreds of straining, thrusting, clumsy pushpots clinging to it and pushing it ever ahead and upward.

It went smoothly toward the east. It continued to gain speed. It did not seem to dip toward the horizon at all. It went on and on, dwindling from a giant to a spot and then to a little dark speck in the sky that still went on and on until even Joe could not pretend to himself that he still saw it. Even then there was probably a tiny droning noise in the air, but nobody who had watched the take-off could possibly hear it.

Then Joe looked at Sally and she at him. And Joe was grinning like an ape with excitement and relief and triumph which was at once his own and that of all his dreams. Sally's eyes were shining and exultant. She hugged him in purest exuberance, crying that the Space Platform was up, was up, was up....

At sundown they were waiting on the porch of the Major's quarters behind the Shed. The Major was there, and Haney and the Chief and Mike and Joe. The Major's whole look had changed. He seemed to have shrunk, and he looked more tired than any man should ever be allowed to get. But his job was done, and the reaction was enough to explain everything. He sat in an easy chair with a glass beside him, and he looked as if nothing on earth could make him move a finger. But nevertheless he was waiting.

Sally came out with a tray. She gravely passed around the glasses and the cakes that went with them. Then she sat down on the porch steps beside Joe. She looked at him and nodded in friendly fashion. And Joe was inordinately approving of Sally, but he felt awkward at showing it too plainly in her father's presence.

Mike said defiantly: "But still it woulda been easier to get it up there if it'd been built for guys like me!"

Nobody contradicted him. He was right. Anyhow every one of them felt too much relaxed and relieved to enter into argument.

Haney said dreamily: "Everything broke right. Everything! They got in a jet stream like they expected, and it gave 'em three hundred miles extra east-speed. They were eight miles up when the pushpots fired their jatos, an' twelve miles up when the pushpots let go—they musta near broke their pilots' necks when they caught their motors again! And the Platform's rockets fired just right, makin' flames a mile long, an' they were goin' then—what were they makin'?"

"Who cares?" asked the Chief peacefully. "Plenty!"

"Six hundred from the pushpots," murmured Haney, frowning, "an' three hundred from the jet stream, and then there was the jatos that all let go at once, an' then there was eight hundred from the earth rotatin'——"

"They had ten per cent of their rockets unfired when they got into their orbit," said Mike authoritatively. "They were two thousand miles up when they passed over India and now they're four thousand miles up and the orbit's stable. This is their third round, isn't it?"

"Will be," said the Chief.

Joe and Sally sat watching the west. The Space Platform went around the Earth from west to east, like Earth's natural moon, but because of its speed it would rise in the west and set in the east six times in every twenty-four hours.

Major Holt spoke suddenly. The austerity had gone out of his manner with his energy. He said quietly: "You four—you gave me the worst scare I've ever had in my life. But do you realize that that sabotage attempt with the two truck-loads of explosive—do you realize that they'd have gotten the Platform if it hadn't been for that crazy trick you four planned, and the precautions we took because of it?"

Joe said depreciatingly: "It was just luck that they happened to pick the same time, and that Haney was up there with those machine-gunners at the right moment. It was good luck, but it was luck."

The Major said effortfully: "There are people called accident

155

prones. Accidents happen all around them, and nobody knows why. You four—perhaps Joe especially—are not accident prones. You seem to be something antithetic to accidents. I would hesitate to credit your usefulness to your brains. Especially Joe's brains. I have known him too long. But—ah—Washington does not look at it in exactly the same way."

Sally touched Joe warningly. But her face was very bright and proud. Joe felt queer.

"Joe," said the Major tiredly, "was an alternate for membership in the Platform's crew. But for penicillin, or something of the sort that made a sick man get well quickly, Joe would be up there in the Platform's orbit now. His—ah—record in the instruction he did take was satisfactory. And—ah—all four of you were very useful in the last stages of the building of the Platform. Again Joe especially. His—ah—co-operation with higher authorities has produced—ah— very favorable comments. So it is felt that he should have some recognition. All of you, of course, but Joe especially. So——"

Joe felt himself going white.

"Joe," said the Major, "is to be offered an appointment as skipper of a ferry rocket, carrying supplies and crew reliefs to the Platform. His rocket will carry a crew of four, including himself. His—ah—recommendations for membership in his crew will have considerable weight."

There was a buzzing in Joe's ears. He wanted to cry and to dance, and especially right then he would have liked very much to kiss Sally. It would have been the only really appropriate way to express his emotions.

Mike said in a fierce, strained voice: "Joe! I can do anything a big elephant of a guy can do, and I only use a quarter of the grub and air! You've got to take me, Joe! You've got to!"

The Chief said benignly: "H'm.... I'm gonna be in charge of the engine room, an' Haney'll be bos'n—let Joe try to take off without us!—an' that don't leave you a rating, Mike, unless you're willin' to be just plain crew!"

Slowly Sally turned her face away from Joe and looked up.

Then they all saw it. A telescope, maybe, would have shown it as the thing they'd worked on and fought for. But it didn't look like

156

that to the naked eye. It was just a tiny speck of incandescence gliding with grave deliberation across the sky. It was a sliver of sunlight, moving as they watched.

There were a good many millions of people watching it, just then, as it floated aloft in emptiness. To some it meant peace and hope and confidence of a serene old age and a life worth living for their children and their children's children. To some it was a fascinating technical achievement. To a few it meant that if wars had ended, and turmoil was no longer the norm of life on earth, this thing would be their destruction. But it meant something to everybody in the world. To the people who had been unable to do anything to help it except to pray for it, perhaps it meant most of all.

Joe said quietly: "We'll be going up there to visit it. All of us."

He realized that Sally's hand was tightly clasped in his. She said: "Me too, Joe?"

"Some day," said Joe, "you too."

He stood up to watch more closely. Sally stood beside him. The others came to look. They made a group on the lawn, as people were grouped everywhere in all the world to gaze up at it.

The Space Platform, a tiny sliver of sunshine, an infinitesimal speck of golden light, moved sedately across the deepening blue toward the east. Toward the night.